Stay up to date with the latest news from Sienna Waters at www.siennawaters.com[1] or by signing up for my newsletter[2].

---

1. http://www.siennawaters.com/

2. http://eepurl.com/dOyZBv

A Big Straight Wedding

Sienna Waters

Published by Sienna Waters, 2021.

To N. –
You hold my heart
xxx

Chapter One

George was clutching her hand under the table, sweat bubbling up between his fingers. The cake was on some kind of trolley, big enough to be wheeled into the restaurant dining room. Bigger than any cake Nic had ever seen. For just a brief second she considered pushing George's face into the thick blue frosting, but the sweatiness of his palms made her take pity on him. Not this time. Not today.

"Happy birthday to you..."

The sound of a hundred voices trying to hit the same note and failing miserably was enough to get Nic to slam her mouth shut and quit singing. She hated this and really, really wished that she hadn't come. As much as she loved George, there was generally only so far she was willing to go for her friends. And attending birthday parties full of old aunts and creepy uncles was definitely over her normal limit. Still, there hadn't really been a choice this time. George could hardly do this alone.

"Are we really going to do this?" George asked from the side of his mouth. Outwardly he was grinning and his sleek blonde hair was perfect and his spray tan was perfect and his teeth were definitely perfect.

"Yes!" Nic hissed back.

George grinned wider, but she could see the strain on his face, the tendons standing out in his neck, as his entire family and half his father's business contacts and a very small handful of friends, those that could be completely trusted only, did their best to serenade him.

"It's going to be fine," Nic whispered. "We've talked about it. We've decided. It's going to be absolutely fine. It's a done deal."

"There'll be no turning back after this," he warned, still grinning like a maniac.

"Good," she said stoutly.

The song ground to a halt and there was a smattering of applause and George leaned forward to blow out the candles, his pants smooth over his tight behind. Nic viewed it dispassionately. It was a nice ass, there was no question about that. The waiter across the room seemed to be admiring it. But it stirred up no sort of feeling for her, no matter how much she tried to imagine her hands on it. It came as kind of a relief, to be honest. Things hadn't changed on the inside at least.

The applause was louder as George managed the feat of blowing out all twenty five candles and then came the cries of "speech, speech!" George shot her a look.

Now or never.

She could see that he was asking her permission one last time.

But there was no decision to be made here. It had already been decided. She gave a curt nod and George turned a shade paler despite his spray tan. He stood up.

"Thank you, thank you for such a lovely party, for showing up, for singing, for being your usual lovely selves."

He was good at this, she gave him that. Good at being in public, good at speaking. Well, he was an actor. Kind of. A waiter really, but he wanted to be an actor. As he spoke, she looked around the room, seeing all eyes on him, except for a bored looking face at the end of the table. She caught Sally's eye. The blue streak in her hair looked out of place among the greys and pearls of George's elderly relatives.

Sally mimed drinking and nodded over at the bar and Nic was about to scrape her chair back, forgetting for a second why she was here, when a hand fell on her shoulder.

Shit.

It was now.

She prepared herself, arranging her face, looking up at George with as much adoration as she could paint there. Even her hands were sweating now.

"And last, but not least, there is a big announcement. The biggest announcement, in fact."

The room held its breath and Nic's head started to swim.

"I'm humbled, proud, nervous, and very, very excited to tell you that yesterday I asked this beautiful woman a very important question."

Nic almost snorted. As far as she could remember the most important question George had asked her yesterday was 'where's the Advil?' closely followed by 'if I ever want Tequila again, will you shoot me?'

"And the answer was yes," he continued. He was beaming down at her and for the first time she understood that he was actually a very good actor indeed. "Nic has agreed to be my wife."

The cheers were loud enough that they had to be breaking some kind of noise ordinance.

"WHAT THE FUCK?"

Sally caught her sleeve as she edged through the crowd to the bathroom, pulling her into a corridor away from prying eyes.

"Uh, I think I'm the one that's supposed to be saying that," hissed Sally. "So, what the fuck?"

Nic raised an eyebrow and shrugged.

"No, no, you don't get to do that. You don't get to suddenly announce your engagement to George in front of your best friend in the whole world who knew absolutely nothing about any of this at all. You don't get to marry George!"

"Why not?" she couldn't help but ask.

"Oh, I don't know. Because he's only twenty five and you're thirty one. I think that six year age gap is going to be a killer. Why not? Why do you think not?"

"He's an attractive guy." She knew she was teasing, putting off the explanation, trying to soothe away the hurt that Sally must feel about not being in the loop.

Sally growled. "You don't get to tell someone that's been tongue-deep in your va-jay-jay that you're marrying an attractive guy. Anyway, George is not attractive. He's fake and tanned and his teeth are capped. Plus, just in case it slipped by you unnoticed, he's gayer than gay. He's so gay that... that..."

"That he can't even think straight?" supplied Nic, helpfully.

"Right."

Nic sighed, keeping one eye on the corridor entrance, hoping that no one could overhear them but equally hoping that someone would come and rescue her from this.

"What's going on, Nic?" asked Sally, more softly, more gently.

"It's an arrangement."

"Yeah, I thought as much." Sally shook her head and the lock of blue at the front of her hair fell into her eyes. She brushed it away. "Nic, you're being an idiot again."

"No, I'm not."

"Yes, you are. I don't even need to know the details here. You're not thinking ahead, not thinking about the consequences, whatever they might be. You're standing up in front of a room full of people and saying that you're going to marry a gay man. How the hell can that possibly end happily?"

"Just trust me," said Nic. She was aching for a drink now.

"You can't do this. You can't just run away when all this goes bad, you know, like you usually do."

"Do not."

"When things got serious with us you disappeared on a bender for three weeks and I found you in a strip bar in Houston."

"Which all worked out for the best in the end," said Nic. "We're much better off as friends, aren't we?"

"Yes, but that's not my point."

"What is your point then?" Nic asked, arching her eyebrow again and desperate for that drink.

"There's so much wrong here that I don't even know where to start," Sally said. Her face was pale, her eyes wide and worried.

"Like what?"

"Like, don't George's family know that he's gay? Like, how the hell are you going to have a straight wedding? Like, how could you lie to so many people at once? Like... so much."

Nic touched her arm. She knew Sally was concerned, knew that she just wanted to help. But this really wasn't helping. She knew what she was doing. For once, there was a clear and very achievable goal in front of her. Something she knew she could succeed at. "I'm going to be fine," she said with real confidence. "Absolutely fine. I promise. I don't have time to go into the details right now. But I'll tell you everything, I swear. And then even you'll see that I'm doing the right thing here."

Doubt dripped from Sally. Nic could feel it in the air. But it wasn't like she wasn't used to being doubted.

"Fine," Sally said, finally. "Fine. I'll trust you for now as long as I get all the gory details later."

Nic grinned. That drink was getting closer, she could smell it. But there was one last thing. Sally was quieter now, the question plain on her face even before she started speaking.

"Why didn't you tell me, Nic?"

Nic took a deep breath and then told the truth. "Because you'd have tried to stop me."

Chapter Two

Klara pushed her keyboard away, disgusted and vaguely sickened by the numbers on her screen. Then she sighed. It was a deep sigh, expending enough air that she choked and coughed until her eyes watered.

"Jesus, I can't even sigh right," she muttered to herself, grabbing a tissue from the box on her desk.

The tissue box was important. You should never underestimate just how emotional people could get about weddings. Sure, she had crying brides, either due to happiness or cold feet. But she also had crying mothers and mothers-in-law, mothers usually had happy tears, mothers-in-law were more likely to have regretful ones in her experience. There was even the odd crying groom.

She smiled, remembering a wedding the previous month. Gavin and Todd were the epitome of gym rats, all toned, tanned and big muscles. They'd also cried more than any other couple she'd ever met. She'd had to replace the tissue box after every appointment with them. Not that she minded. It was cute, adorable really, they were just so in love with each other that they couldn't always hold it in.

The office was as large as she could afford. But it looked smaller. The walls were papered with photographs and fabric samples and invitation ideas, there were stacks of sample books on every available surface. Maybe she should have a clear-out. Maybe that would make her feel better.

She was half-heartedly stacking up yet more sample books and bridal magazines when the door opened.

"Don't bother knocking," she said.

"Wouldn't dream of disturbing you," said Jet. She had a large camera bag slung over her shoulder and a cardboard coffee cup in each hand.

"But just marching in isn't disturbing me at all?"

Jet peered around. "Well, in order to be disturbing you I think you actually have to be doing something. And I don't see any clients around. In fact, you're just standing in the middle of your office with a magazine in your hand. So if anything, I think I'm rescuing you, rather than disturbing you." She held up one hand. "And I brought you coffee."

Klara grinned and took the peace offering. The office coffee machine technically worked, if dripping out pale brown burnt-tasting liquid counted as working, but take-out was so much better.

"So, how's the wedding planning business?" Jet asked, dumping her bag, sagging into a chair and kicking her feet up onto the desk.

Klara snuck a glance at her computer screen. "Don't ask."

"Uh-huh. One of those days, is it?"

"One of those weeks, one of those months, one of those years." She sighed again, making a better job of it this time. At least she didn't end up choking.

"It's a quiet time of year," said Jet.

"Really? For weddings? And where exactly have you just been?" she asked, eyeing Jet's camera bag.

"Ugh. Fine. A wedding."

"One that I didn't plan."

"You don't plan all weddings."

"I'm hardly planning any weddings, which is kind of the point," Klara said. She sipped at her coffee. It was pleasingly warm and tasted of hazelnut.

"Things will get better."

"I wish I could believe you."

Two years. Two years since she'd struck out on her own, leaving a salaried job at one of the biggest and busiest wedding planning studios in the city. And what exactly had she achieved in that time? A packed office and a bank account that was perilously close to empty.

And happiness, she reminded herself. Her eye caught the selection of wedding pictures on her desk, most of them Jet's work. She gave happiness. She worked with happiness every day. She strived to give couples the wedding of their dreams. It was an important job, a fulfilling one.

"Hey, earth to Klara!"

"Yep, sorry, right here. What's up?"

"I was asking about your date." Jet's boots wiggled on her desk top.

Ah. The date. Possibly the reason she wasn't exactly in the brightest of moods today. "It, um, it went."

"It went? What the hell is that supposed to mean?"

Jet shaved her head. A look that Klara was simultaneously shocked by and in awe of. It definitely suited her, though it surprised a fair few clients. And it had the side-effect of making her expressions that much more noticeable. Her heavily lined eyes looked wider, her lips looked redder, and her eyebrows were even more questioning when they arched, as they were currently doing.

"Seriously? You want to go into this now? I'm sitting here heart-broken and you want to grill me on the specifics."

"Since I don't know the specifics, how the hell was I supposed to know that you were heart-broken?" grumbled Jet.

"Fine. We had dinner. It was nice. I walked her to the parking lot. She got in her car and drove off."

"Ugh. Really? No good night kiss? No 'see you next time'? No 'I had a wonderful night'?"

"Nope."

"I thought Julie was supposed to be the love of your life."

"Judy," corrected Klara. "And I never said she was the love of my life."

"You waltzed in here on cloud nine after a brief stop at the deli two blocks away and announced to everyone present that you'd met 'the one.'"

"Everyone present? You mean you?"

Jet took her feet down and turned to face the desk straight on. "I'm sorry it didn't work out."

"Why do I feel like there's a but coming in that sentence?"

"Probably because there is," Jet said. "I'm sorry it didn't work out but... you really need to be more careful, Klara."

"I'm always careful. I met her in a public place and everything."

Jet shook her head. "I meant more careful with your heart. You practically give it away and then wonder why you get hurt all the time. You are the only person I know that has, quite literally, fallen in love at the drop of a hat."

Klara felt her cheeks get warm at the memory of it. She'd been on the metro when the woman across the way from her had dropped her winter hat. They'd both bent at the same time to pick it up and their hands had touched and their eyes had met and... And she'd never seen her again. Despite pining after her for a good month and spending every spare moment she had riding the metro on the same line.

"I'm open minded," she said now. "I'm willing to accept love whenever it appears."

"You're consistently setting yourself up to get hurt," Jet said. "Don't tell me that Julie-Judy just walking away last night didn't sting at least a little."

Tears had pricked her eyes as she'd watched Judy drive away. She'd really thought they had a connection. Not that she was going to admit that now. She shrugged and Jet sighed.

"You know, maybe closing this place down and working somewhere else might be a good thing."

"Don't even think that."

Jet looked at her. "Think about it. You spend all day surrounded by love. It makes sense that you're over-eager to get your share, that you want what you constantly see all the time."

"What's wrong with wanting to fall in love?" She was reaching the end of her coffee and it was getting bitter.

"Absolutely nothing," Jet said. "But giving your heart away for free? That's a recipe for disaster. You need to look after yourself better. You have to give a relationship a chance to develop, and a chance to breathe. You fall in love and then there's nothing else in the world but that person and I can see how that might be suffocating."

Klara screwed her cup up and tossed it into the trash. "So now I'm suffocating?"

Jet groaned. "No. Yes. I don't know. You're... you. You're lovely and pretty and kind and funny and smart, and there's so much to love about you. But I feel like you never give anyone the chance to fall in love with you. You can be... overwhelming."

Jet was her friend. Had been since the day they'd met working the same wedding a decade ago. She was out-spoken, blunt, and occasionally rude. She was also caring and kind and a good friend. Klara blew out her cheeks then nodded. "Okay, okay, you've made your point."

"Just... try not to fall in love so fast, okay?" Jet said. "Take a break. Try and go, like, a month without falling in love. A month without giving your heart away."

Klara rolled her eyes. "Now you're making me sound like a nymphomaniac. I can go a month without falling in love."

Jet drained her own cup and threw it in the garbage. "Really? We'll see about that," she said as she stood up and picked up her bag. "I'll leave you to your book-keeping then."

Klara stood for long enough to kiss Jet's cheek, then went back to her computer. The numbers hadn't grown since the last time she'd looked at them. She rolled her shoulders and got back down to work.

Chapter Three

"Why exactly do I have to do this?"

"Because they're about to be your in-laws and it's polite?" George said as they walked into the restaurant.

"Your parents hate me."

"They don't hate you. Anyway, free food. Just go easy on the wine, okay?"

Nic grunted but followed him to the best table in the house. She didn't need to know the restaurant to know that it was the best table. George's parents always got the best table. That was just the kind of people that they were.

"George, darling," said his mother, grey helmet of hair gleaming in the low light. She kissed him on both cheeks and turned to Nic. "And Nic, of course."

Nic steeled herself for a kiss that didn't come and then was surprised by George Senior's sloppy peck on the cheek.

"We're so glad you could come," Elizabeth Gainer said in a tone that made it very apparent that she was anything but.

Nic smiled a sickly grin and prayed for alcohol. Menus were opened and choices were made and then, finally, a waiter arrived and a drink was within spitting distance. And then came the obvious question.

"So, aren't you going to tell us all about the proposal?"

Nic bit her lip as George launched into the story they'd agreed on.

IT HAD been a Saturday night and they'd been at home in their pajamas drinking out of a sticky bottle of cooking sherry that they'd found at the back of one of the kitchen cupboards. A dreary reality show was on the TV, punctuating their complaints with screams of either ecstasy or pain, it was hard to tell.

"A Saturday night in the city and we're stuck on the couch," George said, sounding truly heart-broken.

"Drinking whatever the hell this is," Nic said, taking another sip. It was sweet enough to make her teeth hurt and she wasn't sure that the alcohol content was high enough to do anything other than give her a headache.

"Better than being sober."

"Debatable," said Nic. She groaned. "How did it come to this?"

"Uh, you spent everything but the rent money buying rounds of B52s last weekend," George reminded her. "And I've been stealing biscotti from work for lunch every day since. I'm going to be enormous by the end of the month."

"You could never be enormous," she said. She glanced over at him in his Scooby Doo pajama pants and a tank-top that showed off the curves of muscles in his arms. "You look fab, Georgie, and you always will."

"Which is why I'll always love you," he said back. "Despite your apparent desire to drive us to bankruptcy."

"Fine, fine," she said, raising her hands in surrender. "I agree that pooling our resources and having a joint budget wasn't the smartest idea in the world."

"Thank God for that."

"You can spend your own pay check next month. On spray tans and gigolos."

"I wouldn't mind a gigolo," George said, laying his head back on the couch and smiling dreamily.

"You are a gigolo," said Nic. "Or maybe you should be."

George stuck his tongue out at her and crossed his eyes and she laughed. He was like the younger brother that she'd never had. Being the youngest of six she was usually the annoying one. It was nice to have someone like George around, someone sweet and funny and irritating. Someone to remind her that life wasn't always serious. As if she was in danger of ever believing that.

"I value my reputation too much to be a gigolo," he said. "Do you think that Spielberg or Tarantino will be impressed if they see that I'm selling this fantastic body for dirty money?"

Nic snorted and picked up her sherry again. "I'd take any kind of money at this point," she said.

The cupboard was quite literally bare. Payday wasn't until Friday, and she wasn't looking forward to a week of scoffing half-eaten sandwiches at the café and hoping that there were stale cakes left over. As the cook she could generally sneak a couple of extra meals home. But every day for a week? That seemed to be pushing it.

"You're the heir to the fortune," she said now, poking George with her foot. "Isn't there a platinum Visa down the back of the sofa or something?"

"Chance would be a fine thing," George said, turning so that his perfect profile was outlined by the light. "Ma and Pa have unequivocally cut me off until I, quote 'get this acting lark out of my system.'"

"Right. Ouch." Nic sniffed and drank again. She was getting used to the taste now. Maybe the sherry was better than nothing. "So, no secret trust funds or anything?"

"Ha, I wish." But the way he stopped with his mouth still half-open captured her attention.

"What?" she pushed, sitting up. "What? Tell me right now."

"Nothing. It's nothing."

"George Raymond Gainer you tell me what exactly you just thought of or I'll give you a wedgie the size of Baltimore."

"Baltimore? Seriously?"

"George..."

He blew out a breath. "There's a trust fund," he said. "Not from my parents though. From my grandmother."

Nic let out a crow of delight. "We're rich! We're finally rich! Caviar in my Ramen from now on."

George rolled his eyes. "Yeah, not quite, darling. The trust fund's a loser, nearly as hateful as the old bat herself. There's no touching the money until I turn twenty five."

"Which is, what, a month and a half from now?" Nic said. Her stomach was flipping. Was this actually going to happen? Not that the money was hers. But having George rich would mean a definite rise in the standard of living around the place. Two-ply toilet paper, for a start.

"Yes," allowed George. "But there's a second condition."

"Which is?" prodded Nic, her heart beating faster now.

"I have to be married."

And her heart slowed down so fast it almost stopped. Her feet were suddenly back on firm ground. "Crap."

"Exactly," George said. He picked up the remote. "I'm switching to National Geographic unless there are any objections?"

Nic shrugged and took another gulp of cooking sherry.

She didn't know why she said it. There was no forethought involved. It was, she supposed later, like most things in her life: spontaneous. Jumping in with both feet without even looking to see if there was water in the pool was the way that George later put it. But so what? That was her, that was how she did things, how she lived life. It was who she was. Do now, regret later. An exciting, if not a particularly sensible, motto.

"You could marry me."

George didn't even look at her. He flicked through TV channels and laughed.

"No," she said. "I'm serious. We could get married. You'd get your trust fund."

He eyed her now. "And you'd get?"

"A rich room-mate," she said. Then she re-considered. "Alright, maybe a percentage of the cash. Like, I don't know, ten percent? What's fair for a fake bride?"

George rolled his eyes. "You'd only spend it on booze and hookers."

"I'd spend it on going to France," she said, again without having put any planning into the words at all. Though now she said them she felt a burning rightness to them. "Going to France to learn how to cook."

"You already know how to cook," he said, turning back to the TV.

"Properly," she said. "I'd learn how to cook properly."

George's attention was being sucked away by a family of meerkats on the screen. Nic sipped at her sticky-sweet glass. And the idea floated around the room, implanting itself into both their brains.

THE MEAL was uncomfortable but free. A pretty fair trade, in Nic's opinion. It was clear as hell that Elizabeth Gainer didn't like her. Whether that was because she was 'stealing' the woman's son away from her or because she was Latina, Nic wasn't quite sure. A mixture of both, she supposed. All the woman had wanted to discuss was wedding plans, and Nic had let her twitter away until she could finally stand no more and had excused herself to go to the bathroom.

She was on her reluctant way back when a hand caught her elbow. She turned to see George Sr. grinning and pulling her to one side.

"Um, what—?"

"Just a moment of your time, my dear."

She didn't have him down as predatory. Handsy, sure, and he definitely looked, but he didn't seem the type to get truly physical. But now she was worried. Confused about what he might want. And that smile was downright creepy.

He cleared his throat as he got her to the bar, out of eyesight of the table.

"Touchy subject," he said.

Nic raised an eyebrow. This didn't sound good. Maybe he knew George was really gay? Maybe he'd had an investigator do a background check on her? Maybe he was in the Klan and about to tell her that anything less than pure white blood wouldn't be acceptable. She gulped.

"But, uh, George has explained a little about your situation."

Nic's heart thudded.

"And, well, I don't want to make a big deal out of this. But I know that you don't have family to speak of."

Not exactly true. She didn't have family to speak *to*. There was a difference. She had a family, they just chose not to acknowledge her or her life choices.

"And, uh, well, I just wanted you to know that Elizabeth and I would like to cover the costs of the wedding."

And a picture crystallized and she understood what was happening and this man, with his beer belly and his shy smile, was suddenly not at all what she had thought. She bent in and hugged him, kissing his cheek as she thanked him as sweetly as she could.

It just went to show what kind of judge of character she really was.

Chapter Four

The very first thing that Klara did every morning was to pick up her phone from the night-stand and check out the engagement announcements.

Not that most people these days felt the need to take out an ad to announce their engagement. In fact, generally only the super-rich or those that were eager social climbers did. And it wasn't like she was going to get any of those kinds of clients anyway. But still, it was a habit. A habit that she'd started because she wanted to be reminded of what *could* happen.

Maybe one day she'd be in a position where she could land one of the big society weddings.

And secretly, in the very back of her mind, she still thought that maybe, one day, she'd be in a position to take out an ad of her very own. *We are pleased to announce the upcoming nuptials of Klara Anne Sorensson and her beautiful fiancée...*

The second name changed weekly. Sometimes daily. Sometimes, if she were really honest, hourly.

As the sun beamed through the window of the cramped little bedroom her fingers slid over her phone and glanced down the list of announcements. She always felt a little skip of happiness in her heart at each set of names. A special skip if it was a same-sex wedding.

There were three major newspapers in the city, and she checked all three. And on this particular morning all three papers featured the same lead announcement.

Mr and Mrs George Gainer Sr. are proud to announce the engagement of their son, George Raymond Gainer Jr. to Ms. Nicolasa Cristina Salinas

To get a wedding like that. What would it be like, she wondered, to work with that kind of budget? If there even was a budget. Maybe it was a free-for-all, maybe it didn't matter how much was spent, as long as the bride and groom were happy. She day-dreamed for a moment about being able to spend as she wished, being able to tend to every detail without compromise.

Then her eyes opened again. It was weird, she thought, that the announcement didn't follow form. Generally, these things listed where the happy couple were from, or at least mentioned the name of the bride's parents.

But the Gainers were the Gainers. They could do as they liked, she supposed. The name was well-known enough in the city that she guessed they set the standards rather than lived by them. George Gainer. Not a family member she recognized. A lesser-known cousin maybe. Still, his engagement merited notice in the papers.

She sighed and stretched and forced herself to put the phone down and get out of bed. The day awaited. And she might not have the Gainer wedding to organize, but that didn't mean that there was nothing to do.

SHE SMILED AT THE WOMAN and tried not to let her cheeks flush. Hard enough given her pale complexion. She hated that her face gave away her emotions so easily.

"I'll take a croissant," she said, aware that her voice had dropped a tone and that she was getting husky. Not planned, of course. It just... it just happened.

"Of course, ma'am. And can I get you anything else with that?"

The woman beamed, her blue eyes shining, her silky hair caught back in a cap. Hands with long, elegant fingers reached for tongs to pick up a plump croissant.

Anything else with that?

A date maybe? A phone number at least?

Klara's mouth dried and her pulse quickened and she smiled as widely as she dared. Emily. That's what the name tag said. Emily. What a beautiful name.

Klara and Emily. She shivered a little at the sound of it. Together it was even more beautiful. Emily and Klara.

"Ma'am?"

Klara blinked to find that Emily was staring at her now, a hint of impatience in her eyes. "Uh, yes, a latte too. To go, please."

She relaxed a little as Emily turned around to face the coffee machine. Emily. She was new, must be new. Klara came into the little bakery every day on her way to the office. And she'd definitely have noticed if there was someone like Emily there.

Just like she'd noticed Carmella at the drugstore, said Jet's voice in her head. Or Linda at the market on the corner. Or Gillian at the pet store down the block. "And you don't even have a pet," Jet had said when she'd heard about that one.

It wasn't that Klara was a nymphomaniac. She truly wasn't. She wasn't out to get laid or to pick women up. Not in the slightest. Okay, okay, she liked sex, but that wasn't the driving force here. The problem ran much, much deeper than that.

If she closed her eyes she could already see Emily's head on the pillow next to hers. She could see the way her hair would be ruffled in the morning. She could see the sweet smile as she lifted the veil at the altar. She could hear the way Emily's light Boston accent would scold their children. She could taste the salt of the sea air as they sat on rocking chairs on the deck of their summer home.

Within milliseconds she could build an entire life around Emily. Around a woman in a bakery that she'd only just met.

"You're in love with the idea of being in love," Jet had once told her.

It was, Klara had to admit, a pretty fair assessment.

But was it so wrong to want someone to share her life with? So wrong to want to finally find her other half? She kept her mind open, that was all. That was her defense. If she didn't try, if she didn't put herself out there then she'd never find the one.

She was very, very careful never to use the phrase 'the one.' She only ever used it in her head. Like a code word for the second name on her wedding invitations. The one.

And the one could be Emily. Of course, it could have been Carmella or Gillian or Julie or Linda or any one of a hundred other women that she'd fallen in love with at first sight.

"Here we are, that'll be nine-seventy."

Emily had turned back and placed a cardboard cup of coffee on the counter and she was smiling and Klara was pulling out her wallet and she was about to speak, about to ask for a number or slide a business card across with her ten-dollar bill. But then she remembered Jet.

A month without giving her heart away.

That had been a joke, surely?

Jet was amazing. Jet was the truest, best friend that she'd ever had. They'd clicked immediately and Klara knew that no matter what happened to her, Jet would be there. Their friendship gave her a safety net, a calm and close feeling that she hadn't had since her parents had died.

The flip side of that was that she was never completely sure when Jet was teasing her and when she was being honest. Take this, not falling in love for a month. It could have been a throw away comment, a joke, a dare, a challenge. Or it could have been honest, simple, effective advice. It was so hard to tell with Jet.

"And here's your change," Emily said.

And she was already turning to the next person in line and the moment was gone. Klara sighed and picked up her coffee. Whether Jet had been joking or not, she'd missed her opportunity. She'd just better hope that Emily hadn't been the one.

Or that she was still working behind the counter a month from now when apparently it would be perfectly okay to throw her heart at strangers again.

SHE WAS putting together a presentation package of tableware and napkins when the phone rang. Clive Albright and his intended, Jessica Shah, hadn't been a demanding couple thus far. But table settings appeared to be their sticking point. Every couple had one. Some couples had more than one. But the fact that the Shah-Albrights couldn't decide on something as simple as a napkin didn't exactly give Klara good feelings about their future.

She was thinking about branching out from the regular creams and pinks and throwing in a pale green tablecloth sample as her hand hovered over the phone. Fine, she decided, adding the green. Maybe they'd both love it. Or maybe they'd both hate it. Either way, at least they'd both agree on something.

"Sorensson Wedding Designs," she said into the phone, eyes scanning through the rest of the tablecloth samples.

"Yes, I'd like to set up an appointment to discuss a wedding," said a voice on the other end of the phone.

Female, older, mother of the bride, Klara guessed. "Of course, ma'am. I'd be happy to meet with you. Did you have a date and time in mind?"

She clicked over to the planner on her computer screen and for the next several minutes they went back and forth over times and places until they found a mutually agreeable arrangement.

"Perfect," she said, putting the information into the computer. "And if I could just have your name?"

"Of course. It's Elizabeth Gainer."

Klara's breath stopped. She'd been wrong, was the only coherent thought in her brain. It was the mother of the groom.

Chapter Five

Nic stretched her feet out under the table and groaned. "Seriously, another one?"

"Maybe you'll like this one," George said as he put a coffee in front of her. "Besides, it's not exactly like this is how I want to be spending my time."

"Fine," Nic said, sitting up properly. "Fair point. So, who's this one then?"

George checked his phone. "Uh, Klara Sorensson of Sorensson Wedding Designs."

"Never heard of them."

"Heard of a lot of wedding planners, have you?" asked George.

"Some," said Nic truculently. "The big names at least. And Sorensson isn't one of the big names."

George grimaced and picked up his cup. "And you're implying...?"

"That your mother arranged this meeting because she doesn't want a big society wedding because she doesn't want you marrying a Latina."

George rolled his eyes. "Listen, Nic. No one's forcing you into this. If you don't want to do it, we won't do it."

She closed her eyes for a second. He was right. No one was forcing her into this. The very opposite. This had been her idea. An idea that for once might actually work. An idea that might give her the kick-start she needed to get on with her life, to make something of herself. And it wasn't as if anyone was actually going to be getting hurt. Not really. Alright, George's parents were going to be spending cash on the wedding, but they could afford it. And she wasn't planning on costing them a bunch anyway.

"Yeah, sorry," she said. "Wedding jitters."

"You need to lay off my mom," said George. "She's my mom. She might not be perfect, but she's mine. And she's really not racist. At least she's never shown that side to me."

"Right, yes, you got it." She'd keep her thoughts about Elizabeth Gainer to herself. She owed George that much.

"So, what are you going to do with your share of the money then?"

It had become one of their favorite past-times. Whenever there was a lull in conversation, whenever the café they both worked at was quiet, whenever one of them needed a reminder about what they were doing and why they were doing it.

"I'm hopping on the first flight to LA, baby," George said.

Nic grinned at him. "I might just join you."

"I thought you were heading to Paris to finally learn to cook!"

"I can go after."

Paris. The idea was growing bigger and bigger now. It was real. More real than she could remember anything being for a long time. Learn how to cook in real style, come back, maybe even open up her own place. That seemed like something she could actually do. A plan that she might even follow through with.

"What if there's no room in my penthouse for you to stay?" George teased.

She reached out and smacked him gently on the back of the head. "There'd better be damn room for me to stay you—"

"Mr. Gainer? Ms. Salinas?"

Her hand was poised for a second slap as she turned to see the newcomer. The wedding planner, she assumed. She could have created a better impression, she should have...

Then all sensible thought disappeared.

Klara Sorensson was tall. Tall and willowy and perfectly formed, like a fairy queen, lithe and elegant in a simple cream dress. Her hair was blonde, brushing her shoulders, bangs hanging into her eyes. And what eyes.

Blue with flecks of green, cat-like, emphasized by a touch of liner and long lashes. She was smiling, a dimple appearing in her cheek. Her mouth was wide and generous, kissable was the word that sprang to mind.

And just like that Nic's body temperature shot up by about ten degrees.

"Nic," she purred, forgetting all about George and holding out her hand.

Klara took it, her fingers cool and long and Nic breathed faster at just the thought of those fingers touching her. The thought of them creeping down her torso, stroking her hips, pushing her thighs apart.

"Klara Sorensson."

Their eyes were locked together, like a circuit had been completed as they shook hands.

Then there was the sound of a throat clearing.

"George Gainer."

Klara's hand dropped Nic's and her face turned to George and the connection was broken. But that didn't stop Nic staring hungrily at the woman as she shook George's hand and deposited a tablet onto the small café table.

"Can I get you a coffee?" George asked.

Klara shook her head and her bangs went into her eyes so that she had to gently blow them back. "No, thanks. Shall we get started?"

KLARA KNEW THAT HER hand was shaking as she passed over the tablet. She couldn't exactly help it. She'd loaded up the wedding pictures already and handing them over to the potential bride and groom was her best plan to get a little respite.

She took a breath, then another as both heads bent over the screen to check out the shots.

"That's pretty nice," George said.

Klara sat back. Her stomach hurt like she was going to throw up, but she knew she wasn't. Her pulse was thready, her heart was beating too fast, and her palms were sweating. All sure signs. Signs that she'd had a hundred times before, of course, but that didn't mean anything. It didn't mean anything at all if this was the one.

Nicolasa Cristina Salinas was not precisely what Klara had been expecting. The leather jacket and skin tight jeans didn't scream 'upper class' or 'society debutante.' Truth be told, the biker boots and white shirt screamed 'lesbian bar' to Klara, but that had to be just wishful thinking.

The one message that she was getting loud and clear though was that Nic was extremely attractive. From the long, curly dark hair, to the flashing dark eyes, to the soft olive skin and the high cheekbones and the swell of her breasts under that shirt and the curve of her thighs in those jeans and... Klara gulped.

"I love the color schemes here," George said, handing back the tablet.

Klara nodded. "Grey and white have been very popular this year," she said. She took another deep breath, trying to clear her head. "If you could maybe give me an idea of what exactly you had in mind?"

"Oh, something small," George said immediately. "Grey and white would be ideal, and then..."

He continued talking but Klara filtered him out. Nic wasn't speaking. Generally, it was the bride that had the clearer idea of what she wanted. It was odd that she wasn't talking. Instead Klara could feel those dark eyes boring into her, could feel them roving over her, could feel them... undressing her?

Jesus. She should have taken the coffee they offered. She was imagining things. Had to be imagining things.

She's straight, you idiot, she said to herself. *She's straight and getting married and you're here to potentially help them, to potentially save your damn company. So quit screwing around and get back on the ball. Get yourself together.*

"Well, that sounds perfect," she found herself saying. "I do offer any services that you may need, and outsource things like photography. I'm happy to take care of absolutely everything with minimal input, or to involve the two of you as much as you'd like to be involved. Some couples want a stress-free experience, others like to know everything. The choice is really up to you."

"Uh, yeah, right," George said.

He was a good looking man. Hell, they were a good looking couple. He had that familiar look, a little too perfect, teeth a little too straight, tan a little too even, a look that Klara usually associated with soap opera actors.

"If you could get me some details, approximate number of guests, food preferences, that sort of thing, I could get you an estimate," she said now, trying desperately to look at George, to keep her eyes away from Nic.

She wanted this, she needed it. Her company needed it. So why was she making such a mess of things? She could feel the opportunity slipping out of her fingers. And all because she'd seen a pretty face. What the hell was her problem? Maybe Jet was right. Maybe she'd be better off out of the wedding business.

George slid a paper across the table to her. "My mother put together a list of information, everything you need to make an estimate should be there. If not, you can call her or me, both our numbers are there. Nic's too, of course."

She allowed herself a glimpse, smiling and nodding at Nic, but the woman wasn't looking at her.

"Perfect," she said, getting up on shaking legs. "I'll get that to you as soon as possible."

She was holding things together, she thought. Just about. She held out her hand again and George took it and they smiled and he thanked her and she thanked him and then she was turning and Nic was there and now she was looking. Her hand was outstretched and Klara had no choice but to take it. It would be rude not to.

She felt a buzzing inside, a flood of warm wetness at the touch of her hand, at those deep brown eyes, at the creak of the leather jacket as Nic shook her hand.

"It's been a pleasure to meet you," Nic said.

It was the only thing she'd said, other than her name. And Klara was sure for a moment that she'd heard a slight emphasis on the word 'pleasure'. No, no, of course she hadn't. She was imagining things.

She snatched her hand back, picked up her tablet and bag, and fled as politely as possible.

Chapter Six

There was a hissing sound as George cleaned out the coffee machine. Nic stuck the mop in the bucket by the door and pulled off her plastic gloves. She was done, finally. And since the place had been quiet all afternoon, she was a good thirty minutes ahead of schedule. She poked her head around the corner.

"All finished in here."

"Gimme a minute and I'll walk out with you," George said. He untied his apron and pulled off his t-shirt, dragging on a slinky looking shirt.

"Looking swish," Nic said, eyeing him. "What's the occasion?"

"Hot date," he grinned. "Tobias, six two, arms thicker around than my legs, and sparkling blue eyes that make you want to do dirty, dirty things to him."

Nic rolled her eyes. "What a thing to say to your future wife."

"Psh, this coming from the woman that was making eyes at a potential wedding planner."

She frowned. She hadn't thought that he'd noticed. Actually, she'd thought that she'd been kind of discreet. Now she was worried that Klara the wedding planner might have noticed too. "Was not," she said, though it sounded kind of feeble.

"Bullshit," said George as he finished buttoning his suit. "And it's playing with fire, you know that, right? I'm pretty sure that sleeping with a wedding planner is going to end in trouble. Which is exactly why I'm voting for the first option. Dream Weddings or whatever the damn place was called."

Nic groaned. "No, come on. They were like the McDonald's of weddings, they were so smooth and they cost a damn fortune."

"You're not paying for it."

True, but George Sr. was and she was damned if she'd cost him a fortune. Anyway, there'd been something about Klara, something she'd liked aside from the fact that she was attractive. Which she was. Very. There was a rumble in her stomach that might have been hunger but was more probably a reminder of just how attractive she'd found Klara.

There had been a little nervousness there, some courage, a sense that Klara needed the job. And she was all about giving people who needed it a chance. She checked her phone. There was no time to argue about this now.

"I gotta run," she said. "And we're not making decisions until the estimates come in. We're definitely not making them without agreeing first, right?"

George rolled his eyes but nodded. "Fine, fine." He picked up his bag and gave a wide grin. "Alright baby, don't wait up."

"Like I ever do," she said as she watched him head out of the café.

She wondered if this Tobias would be the one. George dated a lot, for sure, but he rarely got too excited about a man. And when he did, he fell hard. She got the sense that Tobias might just be one of the falling hard cases. She shook her head, hoping like hell that George wasn't about to bust their plan, wasn't about to make things difficult for them both.

THE BAR WAS QUIET, making it an unusual choice for Sally. Nic walked in and saw her friend immediately, waving like a maniac from a seat at the back. She made her way over, dropping her purse on a bench seat and sliding into the booth.

"This place is deader than my bed on a Wednesday night."

"Deliberately so," Sally said. She glared at Nic. "Don't think that I've forgiven you for getting engaged, I haven't. And the only reason we're here right now is so that you can give me the explanations that I deserve."

"Thus explaining the lack of noisy crowds and high volume music," Nic said, cottoning on.

"Exactly. So order your drink and get talking, girl."

Nic beckoned over a waiter and ordered herself a beer before she settled more comfortably into her seat. "So, what do you want to know?"

"Well, why don't we start with the fact that you're gay, he's gay, you're getting married and everyone in that restaurant where you announced it seemed to think that that was perfectly okay."

Nic laughed. "Yeah, okay, okay, you're owed some explanations, I get it." A beer appeared in front of her. "Alright, so it was kind of my idea, I guess."

Quickly and succinctly she laid out what had happened. But when she was done, Sally was still frowning in confusion.

"Okay, I mean I suppose I get that there's money involved. But I refer to my previous question. George's parents and family have no idea he's gay? Or they think he just switched sides over night?"

Nic scratched her nose. "He never told them," she said. "That's not exactly true. He told his parents that he was bisexual, said it was easier that way. Technically, it's true, he did have a girlfriend in high school. He said he planned on telling them if anything got serious with a guy, but it never did and so..."

"And so he's never come clean about it," Sally said. "Alright. I supposed that's understandable. Not exactly commendable, but understandable. So the plan is that you're both going to rip an old lady off then?"

Jesus. She was going to need another beer for this. She gestured for one. She loved Sal to death, had known her for years now. Sally had been one of her very first girlfriends when she moved to the city and she couldn't imagine life without her in it. Sal was also incredibly judgmental and had a tendency to cut straight to the heart of the matter, though Nic knew she was coming from a place of concern.

"She's an old lady," Nic agreed. "But by all accounts she's a bit of a witch. And the money's in a trust fund, it's not like we're taking it out of her hands."

"But you do have to get married."

"Inescapably yes," Nic said. "The terms of the fund specify that George has to be twenty five and married. Married to a woman, that is. The pronouns are there, the word wife is used, we've had a lawyer check everything over and it's just the way it is. The money's a private fund and the owner of the fund is allowed to put whatever strictures they like onto it."

"That's stupid."

"I agree," said Nic, shrugging. "It's some family thing. Apparently the grandmother's brother wasted his inheritance on crack and rent boys or something and so she and her late husband made it tougher for the next generations to get to their trust funds. Not a lot we can do about it."

"So if George doesn't get married, the money just sits there?"

"Haven't really thought about it, but I guess so." Nic sat forward, hands wrapped around her bottle. "I know, it all seems crazy, it sounds stupid, insane even. But it's not that bad once you think about it. The money should be George's, it's his and it shouldn't matter whether he's married or not. I'm just helping out a little is all."

"With no thought of yourself." Sally arched an eyebrow.

"Sure, I get my share," said Nic.

Sally sighed and shook her head. "Are you really sure about doing this?"

"Yes," said Nic. "Absolutely and completely sure. I don't see that it's a bad thing."

"You wouldn't."

She bit back a prick of anger. "What's that supposed to mean?"

"I mean that you're terrible about thinking of consequences, Nic. I'm not telling you anything you don't already know. You're impulsive, spontaneous, and you tend to forget that your actions have repercussions. Like when you picked up that puppy in front of the grocery store."

"I saved him!"

"Yes, and after two weeks you had to find him a new home because you hadn't considered the fact that he needed expensive food and walks twice a day when you were working fourteen hour shifts."

Nic bit her lip. Fair point. "George isn't a puppy."

"I know he's not. I'm just worried that you might be getting in over your head here because you haven't thought things through."

Sal's eyes were worried and the lights from the bar caught the blue streak in her hair and made it glow and Nic reached out and took her hand. "I know you're worried about me. But I'm fine. Really. I promise. George and I talked about this for weeks before we decided to do it."

"And of course it's George that drags you into this."

"I know he's not your favorite person in the world, but he's a good guy. And he deserves his trust fund, despite that fact that without me he's unlikely to marry a woman, don't you think?"

"I guess," Sally said.

"Right then. So let's have a drink and you can congratulate me and then we can talk about your bridesmaid's dress."

Sally was half-way through a nod before she caught up with what was going on. "A dress?"

"Well, you're going to be my bridesmaid, aren't you?"

"A bridesmaid at a sham wedding where my ex-girlfriend is marrying a very gay man to get money from an old lady."

"Don't say I don't bring excitement to your life," Nic said with a grin.

Sally shook her head but she was smiling. "Fine, fine," she said. "As long as I don't have to wear pink."

"I'll be sure to tell the wedding planner," promised Nic.

And a shiver of anticipation ran through her. Just how, she wondered, was she going to persuade George that Klara was the planner to hire? More beers came. She'd have to work on the Klara Sorensson issue later...

Chapter Seven

Klara shifted a pile of tablecloth books over a few inches and swiped ineffectively with a duster. She coughed as the dust rose up to meet her throat. Cleaning was a procrastination, she knew that. It was a way to not think, or a way to think no further ahead than whether or not she actually had to move furniture to vacuum. And to be fair, the office did need a good clean.

Still though. She did know that she was trying not to think.

And it was almost working. Almost until the door slammed open and Jet exploded in, camera bags flying.

"So, are we in? Do we get the Gainer wedding? Should I buy a new dress? Spruce up my portfolio? Come on, tell me all!"

"I might if you let me get a word in edgeways," Klara said, still sniffing from the dust. She was deliberately not looking at Jet, but the silence stretched longer and longer until there was a huff of disgust.

"You blew it, didn't you?"

"Did not!" She was so stung by the accusation that she turned around. Jet was lounging in her desk chair. "I didn't."

"So we're in the running then?"

Klara nodded and put her cleaning rag down. "We're in the running."

"Um, you could sound a little more excited about this, you know?"

"Could I?"

"A big society wedding, huge budget, I'm guessing. And even if not, it'll definitely get your name out there. This is the break you've been waiting for, Klar. You rock this wedding and you'll be hitting the big time. No more business worries, no more number crunching, no more freelance photographers."

Klara dumped herself onto the small, pink sofa. "I wouldn't fire you."

"I was thinking more along the lines of you could hire me," said Jet. "You know, give me a salary, health insurance, that kind of jazz."

Klara managed a weak smile. "Yeah, maybe."

Finally, Jet's eyes narrowed. She ran a hand over her shaved head, then sighed. "Wanna tell me what's going on?"

She closed her eyes. She really didn't. She really didn't want to talk about it or think about it but with Jet here her chances of forgetting all about the stupid interview were slim to none. Maybe it was better to face facts.

"I can't do the wedding."

There. She'd said it. The horror that had been lurking in her brain for the last forty-eight hours. Okay, she'd done as she'd promised. She'd put together an estimate automatically, working like a robot, not thinking about names or faces, just the numbers. She'd even sent it, though when she looked back she knew she'd quoted too much.

But now she'd said what she'd known from the second she'd touched Nicolasa Salinas's hand. There was no way in hell she could take this wedding.

"Why the hell not?"

Jet sounded mad, and she had every right to be. Jet would profit from landing the Gainer wedding just as much as she would. She turned miserably to her best friend, not wanting to admit her own weakness.

"Well," poked Jet. "Why not?"

"I just can't."

"Not good enough. This is the chance of a lifetime, you're going to need to do better than that. Are they complete assholes?"

Klara shook her head.

"Um, I don't know... Racists? Homophobes? Wait, I know, did he hit on you when she was in the bathroom?"

"No!"

"Wouldn't be the first time," Jet said.

Which was true. Grooms weren't always as well behaved as she'd like. And groomsmen definitely weren't. "It's not that."

"It's not him," Jet said, thinking, a crease between her eyebrows. Then her eyes opened wide. "It's her."

Klara bit her lip, said nothing.

"Jesus, Klar. Seriously? You've got the hots for the bride? *That's* why you can't do the wedding?"

Klara gave the smallest nod possible. And Jet leaned back in the desk chair and watched her for a second. Then she snorted. "So, you only agree to do weddings with unattractive brides, is that the deal?"

"Of course not!"

"Then why is this a problem?" Jet asked. "I mean, it must have happened before and you got over it."

"Nope, never."

Jet snorted again. "Right. You, the girl that falls in love fifty times a day has never had a crush on any of the beautiful brides that surround her on a daily basis."

"Nope," Klara said again. Jet just stared at her. "No, really, I never have. It's the truth."

"How is that even possible?"

She shrugged. "It's different. They're happy, they're part of a couple already, they come to me to complete their happiness. It's like... like I don't even see them as women maybe. They're not possible mates, they're already brides. It's hard to explain. But I swear to you that I have never, not once, had a crush on any of the brides that I've worked with."

"Until now."

"Until now," she echoed.

"What changed?"

"No clue. It just... It just happened."

But that wasn't exactly true, was it? There had been something off about the Gainer wedding from the very beginning. Something just not quite right. And that feeling had only gotten worse when she'd met the happy couple. The attractive, made for each other, perfect couple that now that she came to think of it hadn't seemed that happy at all. Actually, they'd seemed more irritated, slightly bored even.

Jet shook her head. "Klara, you need to think very carefully about this. I know what you're like, so do you, just because you have momentary feelings for someone doesn't mean that you have to act on them. Getting this wedding would be a huge chance. You can't turn it down just because... well, because you think that maybe, possibly you might have feelings for someone you've met for all of ten minutes."

Klara bit her lip again. Jet was right. Of course she was right. She nodded and Jet's phone beeped and then she was picking up her bags again.

"I gotta run. Think about it, Klara. Don't do anything rash, okay?"

"Okay."

And then she was gone and Klara was left sitting on the sofa alone.

Obviously, Jet was right. She'd literally just met Nic. Nic was the bride, she was unattainable and completely off limits. And Klara was an adult. She could restrain herself, stop herself speaking, touching, smelling... She gulped.

When she closed her eyes she could smell the musk of Nic's leather jacket, could feel the touch of her hand. She blinked her eyes open again. She had to stop this. It was ridiculous.

When she was seven years old she had found a big, fat book in her parents' bedroom. It had been a rainy day during the summer vacations and she'd been bored and restless. And when she found the book she'd been curious enough to open it, though books and words had never been her thing.

Inside she'd found pictures covered with delicate tissue paper. The smell of flowers, the delicacy of the paper, had entranced her and she knew suddenly that she'd found something very, very special. It was a long moment before she could persuade herself to lift the tissue, she was so afraid of spoiling it, tearing it.

Her fingers trembled as she finally moved it to one side, revealing a picture that just about took her breath away.

The woman was in profile, her face tilted up to look at the man. Klara was seven, not stupid, she knew immediately that this was a wedding portrait, the clothes, the lacy veil gave it away. What she wasn't prepared for were the looks on the faces of the man and the woman. Such happiness, such completeness, such absolute contentedness. Even then, so young, she'd stared at the picture for long minutes, longing after those feelings, knowing it was all she wanted for herself.

It wasn't until she was already reaching to turn the tissue paper back, to cover the precious photograph, that she realized the people were her parents, could only be her parents. And it was such a revelation to her. That normal people could have those feelings, that the joy, the completeness weren't reserved for princesses or fairies or movie stars, but they were floating around out there ready for just anyone to take.

And it was all she'd searched for ever since.

She sucked in a breath now and swallowed. Something was off with the Gainer wedding, she knew that. And she had a sense of danger. Something was warning her off, something was telling her that this would be more trouble than it was worth. Something was shaking her and telling her to back off.

She was very good at ignoring herself when she had to. Part of her longed to see Nic again, to get close to her, to touch her, to talk to her, to laugh with her. The far more sensible part of her wanted to run a mile.

She picked up her cleaning rag again. She had no idea what she was going to do. But then, she thought as she started dusting, probably the decision would be made for her. Probably she wasn't going to get the wedding anyway. They'd choose one of the big studios and she'd never have to worry about seeing Nic ever again.

Chapter Eight

"I don't want a big wedding studio!"

George took a step back, as though blown away by the strength of her voice. "Okay..." he said, slowly. "Um, why?"

Nic looked down at the four estimates that were lying on the coffee table. Klara's was by far the lowest. Yes, she wanted to see the blonde. Even though she understood that probably she should do nothing about the attraction she felt for her. More importantly just at the moment though, Klara's estimate was by far the lowest of the four.

"Klara's cheapest."

"Not really an issue," George reminded her.

"Yes, yes it is. Your parents are paying for this," she said. "And we're deceiving them enough as it is."

"Nic, this isn't a question of money."

But it kind of was for her. Partly. George Sr. had been sweet and she'd been touched when he'd taken her aside to tell her he wanted to pay for the wedding. Touched enough that for an instant she'd felt terrible about lying to him. And she was determined not to rip him off, no matter what George said about money not being important.

"I don't want a big studio dealing with things," she said again.

"It'll be faster, less effort, less for us to do," said George. "We'll just hand over our requirements and then show up for the ceremony. Done and dusted."

Maybe that was the problem. Maybe she wanted someone else there, someone that understood things, someone like Klara, someone who could hold her hand as all this crazy wedding stuff took flight. Maybe she needed a little support. Maybe she wasn't quite as confident an actor as George was.

"Klara said she could handle everything," she pointed out.

George shook his head. "Nic, why do you even care? I mean, it's not like we're really getting married, it's not like this is your one chance to do this right. You—"

"Maybe it is," she said.

He shut up and looked at her and she regretted saying what she'd said. But she was saved by the bell, literally. Her phone alarm buzzed and then rang and she picked up her jacket from the back of the sofa.

"We need to run if we're going to make our shifts," she said.

George hesitated and then nodded. "Fine, we can talk about this later. But we need to make the decision today, right? No point in prolonging things."

"Right," said Nic. She walked ahead of him to the front door, letting them both out of the apartment. Then she looped her arm in his. "So," she said in conciliatory fashion. "Why don't you tell me all about Tobias and his monster arms."

"He doesn't only have monster arms," George said with a devilish grin.

Nic snorted with laughter and pulled him closer as they walked down the street toward the café.

SHE WAS loading the bottom drawer of the dishwasher when she heard movement in the kitchen. Straightening up she was just in time to see Danny, the youngest of the waiters, pop the remains of a half-eaten donut into his mouth. He flushed red when he saw her watching.

"Hey, no judgment here," she said quickly. God knows, she'd eaten scraps from plates often enough herself. With a quick hand she reached over and closed the sandwich press on top of the pre-prepared ham and cheese toastie inside.

"Sorry," Danny said, swallowing quickly. "Sorry. It won't happen again. Disgusting, I know."

Her eyes darted to the pass, there were no orders waiting, so she leaned up against the dishwasher, folding her arms.

"Wanna tell me about it?"

Danny blushed even brighter red. "Nothing to tell," he said.

She shook her head. "Bullshit. Let me guess. Broke as hell, no spare cash for food, so hungry that you can barely stand upright and no hope of food until next pay-day."

His eyes darted away and she knew that she was right. The sandwich maker beeped and she opened it, pulled out the hot toastie onto a plate, and offered it to Danny. He took it with only a second of hesitation, fast enough to tell her that he was truly hungry.

She was silent until he'd devoured the sandwich. Then she tried again. "Wanna tell me about it?"

He wiped his mouth on the back of his hand, then nodded. "Got thrown out."

She nodded.

"It, uh, was just me and my mom for a long time. Then she met this guy, Luke. He's a tool. He, um, he yells a lot. Obviously doesn't like me, I'm in the way. But it's how things go, and for a while it was okay. I mean, not great, but I could put up with it. Then he slapped her."

"Right," said Nic, knowing where this was going.

"I stepped in, he handed me my ass on a plate and..." He looked away from her and she knew that he was struggling not to cry and she gave him his moment. When he turned back his eyes were dry. "I just thought that she'd choose me, you know?"

"I know," Nic said, heart breaking. "You got a place to sleep? Somewhere safe?"

Danny nodded. "I'm crashing on a friend's couch. I can stay as long as I like, not a problem there. Got a roof over my head and a hot shower every night. Which makes me lucky, I guess."

"How old are you?"

"Seventeen." He guessed her next question. "I graduate in two months. Things'll get better after that."

She couldn't help but wonder if they really would. She hoped for his sake they would, but she knew the odds out there. She'd been out there herself. And she hadn't always been lucky enough to have a couch to sleep on.

Stepping around Danny she reached for her backpack and pulled her wallet out of it. There was a twenty and a ten. All she had until pay-day on Friday. But there was plenty of food here, and the fridge at home was half-full. She took out the twenty and handed it over.

"I don't need hand-outs."

"Yes, kiddo, you do. And it's nothing to be ashamed of. You can pay me back when you're rich and famous."

"I—"

"Get out of here," she interrupted. "Before the customers get crazy and you lose the only job you've got. Go on, back on the floor."

He shot her a grin as he left, the door swinging behind him, letting George slip into the kitchen on the back-swing. He walked right up to her, hugged her close enough that she could feel the beating of his heart.

"Choose any wedding planner you like," he said in her ear.

She pulled back. "Really? Help a homeless kid and I get to make my own wedding decisions? Is that how it works?"

"No," he said. "Show me how much of an idiot I can be and then you get to make your own wedding decisions. That's how it works."

"Not a clue what you're talking about," she said, turning back to the dishwasher and pushing buttons.

"You said this might be your only chance," he said to her back. "And I think you really believe that. You really believe that this little show we're putting on might be your only shot at getting a wedding."

"Might be."

There was a beat of silence. "It won't, Nic. I know you can't always believe that, but I believe it for you. You've been through a lot of shit, but that's only going to make the ending even sweeter."

She turned now. "Right, happy endings, because life has so many of those, right?"

George shrugged. "If you don't believe in that, then what's the point?"

"George—"

"You don't want to be let down again," he said. "I get that. Your family were supposed to be there for you and you dare to tell them who you really are and they disappear into the woodwork. You don't want to believe in anything again, just in case it doesn't come true."

"Armchair psychologist now, are we?" she said, but she wasn't looking him in the eye.

"I'll be there for you, Nic. And one day, you'll find someone else who will be. You'll find someone else that sees what's inside that crusty, commitment-phobic exterior, someone who doesn't believe that you're spontaneous to be exciting, but sees that you're spontaneous because you're scared of anything that lasts longer than a minute. Scared of letting yourself be yourself. Scared of opening up. And when you find that person, you'll get your real wedding."

She said nothing for a minute. She couldn't. Her throat was tight and her eyes stung and she had to swallow hard to push all the emotion back down again. "Okay," was all she could find to say when she could speak.

"In the meantime," he said. "Consider this your dress rehearsal, good practice for when you're going to do the real thing." He hugged her from behind. "And choose whichever wedding planner you'd like."

Chapter Nine

The day started with a brown envelope. No good day ever starts with a brown envelope. Klara clutched the envelope in her teeth as she held coffee in one hand and tried to re-lock the mailbox with her other hand. So by the time she got into the office, it was a slightly soggy brown envelope. She propped it up on her desk and eyed it while she drank her coffee.

She could open it immediately and get it over with. Like ripping off a band-aid. Or she could let it sit and fester for a while and work her way up to it. She sipped at her hazelnut latte and considered her options.

Emily had not been working this morning, which was probably a good thing. Good in that she hadn't been tempted to hand out her phone number. Or, now that she was thinking about it, maybe a bad thing because now she had nothing to take her mind off Nic.

There had been some quite disturbing dreams the night before, and she wriggled in her chair a little at the memory of them. Dreams that were quite inappropriate to have about a potential client, a future bride, and a definitely straight woman. It wasn't like she could control her sub-conscious, but she did wish it could be a little more co-operative.

More than a week had passed though, and she knew now that it was unlikely she was going to get the job. Most contracts were signed either immediately or within a day or so, so it was looking like the Gainer wedding was going elsewhere. For the best, she told herself. But she couldn't stop disappointment bubbling in her chest.

It *was* for the best. She wouldn't have to deal with whatever these weird, insistent emotions were that she was feeling for Nic. She'd grown comfortable with calling her Nic in her head, like they were friends already. On the other hand, it was complete crap for business. She was keeping her head above water, but only just. One more wave and she'd be drowning.

Another sip of coffee and she gave in, reaching for the envelope. 'Eating the frog for breakfast,' was what her father had called it. If the worst thing you have to do all day is eat a frog, then you should eat it for breakfast, that way the rest of your day is free and clear. She took a deep breath and ripped the envelope open across its soggy edge.

Just as she was withdrawing the letter inside though, a knock sounded at the door. She frowned. Not Jet, she never knocked like that. And she had no appointments this morning. Her heart thrummed. Perhaps it was Nic, perhaps they'd decided to give her the wedding after all. Or perhaps Nic had ditched George, finally come to her senses, realized that what she needed was Klara... For God's sake.

"Come in," she shouted, before the fantasy could take her any further.

"I hope I'm not disturbing anything?"

The woman that walked in was absolutely stunning. Jessica Shah was tall, lithe, had skin like toasted almonds, and eyes so deep and dark that you could fall into them. A waterfall of thick, black hair fell down to her waist.

"Not at all," Klara said, standing up. "We didn't have an appointment, did we?"

"Er, no. No, we didn't," Jessica was uncharacteristically subdued. "Do you think I could sit?"

"Of course," Klara said. Something was wrong, it was more than evident. Jessica's eyes were rimmed with pink, her voice had a blocked-up quality about it. Instinctively, Klara moved the tissue box so it was a little closer to the woman.

Jessica sank into the chair and smiled weakly at Klara and Klara knew what was about to happen, or had a fair idea. It happened. People got cold feet, people cheated, people changed their minds. On one occasion that she could remember, one party had decided that joining a monastery was preferable to marriage. It was the flip-side to working in the wedding industry: not every happy wedding ended up being happy or a wedding. The only question here was whether this was pre-wedding nerves, or the real deal.

"This is terribly difficult," Jessica said, her accent carrying clipped British consonants.

"Take your time," Klara said. "There's no hurry. Would you like some coffee?" She remembered the British accent. "Or tea?" she added.

Jessica obviously steeled herself, sitting up straighter, shaking her head. "No, thank you. I'm afraid that Clive and I will be canceling the wedding."

Klara arranged her face into a look of sympathy. She hated this part of the job, hated that true love had to come so hard to some people. But secretly on this occasion she couldn't help but think that Jessica was doing the right thing. Sure, the couple had looked happy at the start but they literally hadn't been able to agree on a tablecloth and she hadn't foreseen the marriage lasting particularly long.

To be honest, Clive Albright had been punching far above his weight. Whilst Jessica was stunning, Clive was a balding middle aged man with a gold tooth and a thick wallet. Klara had drawn her own conclusions about the couple, but had kept them private. She tried not to judge, but it was occasionally hard. At least Jessica had seen the light now, could move on, could find someone worthy of her.

"I'm so sorry," she said, inching the tissue box closer.

"I don't know what to do," Jessica said, holding on by a thread. "I can't believe he'd leave me like this."

"*He* left *you*?" Klara said before she could stop herself.

Jessica nodded miserably. "Said he didn't want to be tied down, couldn't commit to one woman. And I'd tried so hard to make him happy."

Really, she had to remember not to judge. Jessica was close to tears and despite what she'd said, Klara got up and put the kettle on. The woman needed tea.

IT WAS two hours before Jessica Shah finally left, with promises that Klara would cancel everything that needed canceling and that everything but the deposit would be returned. Not exactly great for business.

Strike that, Klara thought with a groan. A disaster for business.

The Albright-Shah wedding had been a big one, plenty of relatives attending, big expectations and a big budget to match. Now that it was canceled not only was there a hole in her diary, but her bank account was going to be down to practically nothing.

She had to figure out a way out of this. For the first time she was actually worried that this whole project would come crashing down around her ears. And what would she do if she didn't plan weddings? It wasn't like she had a heap of qualifications and a huge inheritance to fall back on.

She had a college English degree, some specialized diplomas from weekend workshops, and a handful of internships at wedding companies. That was it. And as for inheritance, she'd poured whatever was left over after selling her parents' house into the business already. There was quite literally nothing else. Not a bean.

She tried to imagine herself somewhere else, doing something else, and just couldn't. Even after a decade, each and every wedding she planned and attended was just as touching, just as beautiful as the first. She still wanted this.

The stupid brown envelope was still on the desk and she ripped the letter out of it, casting her eyes down the text and then groaning aloud. A seventy dollar monthly rent increase on the office. Fantastic. Amazing. Just what she needed.

Really, could this day get any worse?

Maybe she should lock up shop and go home. Get into a hot shower, drag her PJs on, make hot chocolate and watch the Hallmark channel until the day was over. She could start over tomorrow, could deal with all this, come up with a plan tomorrow.

She'd just about convinced herself to play hooky for the rest of the day when the phone rang.

"Sorensson Wedding Designs," she said out of habit.

"Ah, yes, is that Klara?"

"It sure is," she said, bending to get her purse from under the desk. The sooner she got out of here the better.

"This is Nic Salinas. We met last week?"

She shot up so fast that she cracked her head on the desk and tears flooded her eyes. She bit her tongue in an effort not to cry out. "Uh, yes, of course," she managed to say without sounding like she'd just given herself a concussion.

"Well, if it's still possible, we'd love for you to plan our wedding."

Klara rubbed at the growing bump on her head. Nic's voice was deep and captivating and she could imagine her reading goodnight stories, could imagine her purring in her ear, could... She really shouldn't take this wedding. Really, really shouldn't.

"Klara? Are you still there?"

"Yes, I'm here," she said quickly.

"So, can you send me the contract and I'll get it signed?"

She shouldn't but Jessica had just canceled her wedding and the rent was going up and it had already been such a shitty day and this could just be the one thing to save her day, to save her business. How could she say no?

"I'll email it to you right now," she said, already opening up the browser on her computer. "What's your address?"

Nic told her, carefully spelling it out and Klara's hands were shaking as she typed and then sent out the contract.

"All sent."

"And... I got it," Nic said. "Do you need just my signature, or both of us or...?"

"Just yours is fine," Klara said, amazed that her voice was so steady.

"Then you'll have this back in five minutes," said Nic. "Let me get onto this and then we can arrange a meeting to get things started."

"Sure," Klara squeaked.

Nic hung up and Klara sat back and her head throbbed and her pulse raced and her eyes closed and what had she just done? She sighed. She'd just have to behave herself. Be a professional. She needed the business. Her hand went up to her head again. Besides, she could always blame the bump on the head if things went south, right?

Chapter Ten

There was no way that Nic would admit that she was nervous. Not even to herself. Okay, her palms were sweating, but that was probably just the unseasonably warm morning. And her stomach felt flippy and weird, but then those eggs at breakfast hadn't smelled too fresh, so that was probably it.

She flipped her hair over her shoulder, aware of the sweet, clean scent of shampoo and walked toward the end of the block. She had the address, she knew where she was going, she just didn't really know what to expect.

Which was why she could be nervous if she was, which she definitely wasn't. She didn't know what to expect, what was expected of her, she just knew that she had to help plan a wedding. A wedding that would convince George's family they were in love and deserving of his trust fund, and maybe, as a small side effect, might make his mother like her just a little more.

She was on no account nervous because she was about to see Klara. Because she wasn't nervous. And also because there was no way that a long, lean, blonde, delicious woman like Klara would ever make her nervous. No woman made her nervous. Ever. She knew what she was doing and knew what she wanted, there was no reason to be afraid of a woman.

Her hand was sweaty enough that she had to wipe it on her jeans before she knocked on the door.

"Nic, how lovely to see you, come on in."

It was like being punched in the stomach, and Nic knew exactly how being punched in the stomach felt. Klara opened the door, smiled, blew her bangs out of her eyes, and Nic's core melted. Jesus, there was something about her. For maybe the first time she thought that perhaps George had been right, perhaps this was playing with fire, perhaps she should have gone with the bigger company.

"Can I get you anything?" Klara asked.

Nic let herself be led into a room that was crowded with books and folders and binders, pictures littering the walls, full but comfortable, messy but homely. There was the scent of lemon and polish.

"Uh, coffee would be good, thanks."

"I'm warning you that it's not the best coffee in the world."

"As long as it's hot and caffeinated, it's fine." Anything to get Klara to step away for a moment, to give her time to think, to breathe.

Alone in the room, she studied the pictures on the walls. Happy couples all of them. She wondered idly what it would feel like to be in a relationship like that, so true and honest and, well, legit. Having someone always there for you.

"Here you are."

Klara laid a hand on her shoulder as she placed a coffee cup in front of her and Nic froze still. The heat from the connection flushed through her body. Jesus, she had it bad this time. She really couldn't sleep with a wedding planner. Not when the planner in question was planning her own wedding, right? Bad plan, right?

"Uh, you must have been to lots of weddings?" Nic said inanely. It wasn't usually hard to make conversation.

"You could say that," Klara said. She sat down behind her desk and Nic followed, taking the chair opposite her. "I see about one a week in the busy season."

"Jesus. Don't you get sick of them?"

Klara grinned and her teeth were perfect and white and that dimple showed again. "Never."

Nic studied her, she was telling the truth. She could imagine kissing her, imagine that head thrown back in ecstasy. A thrill went through her. "You see all kinds of couples though."

"That I do. Old, young, straight, gay, mixed, even an arranged marriage or two. It takes all sorts."

"So you must have a sense of whether things will work out or not?" She was getting curious now, the conversation coming more easily.

"Sure I do."

Nic nodded and arched an eyebrow. "What about me and George?" she couldn't help but ask.

"No comment."

"Diplomatic," laughed Nic.

The answer had made her like Klara more. Yes, there was definitely a physical attraction. But she could just have said 'you're a great couple,' or 'obviously you guys are going to make it.' She didn't though. She had a sense of humor, she wasn't a liar, her eyes had twinkled when she'd said 'no comment.'

There was more to Klara than just a pretty face and Nic found that intriguing. Found her intriguing. She leaned forward and was about to ask another question, but Klara got in first.

"So, shall we get down to work then?"

Nic bit her tongue, then sat back and nodded. "Work it is," she said.

"WE HAVE PICTURES HERE," Klara said.

She got up from her desk and found the appropriate binder, planning on bringing it back to the desk. But the next thing she knew, Nic had moved too and was standing right next to her. With a gulp, Klara turned the pages, letting Nic lean in to see pictures of dress designs.

Her eyes darted sideways. Barely an inch separated them. She could smell the herbal scent of Nic's shampoo. She could see the delicate hairs on her cheeks, could feel the warmth of her.

Something was pounding inside her and it took a second to realize it was her pulse. She ached to inch closer to Nic and had to hold herself back.

The physical attraction was certainly there. Something magnetic, something primal and hormonal and biological had her wanting to get closer, wanting to touch and taste and smell.

She needed to get laid.

That was all.

It had been a few months, she'd probably be like this around anyone. She needed to get out more and get a date. Maybe Emily from the bakery. She'd ask her tomorrow morning, no matter what she'd told Jet about not giving her heart away for a month.

"I like this one," Nic said.

She brought her arm up to point and it brushed against Klara's side. She jumped back as though electrocuted.

"You have plenty of time to decide on a dress," she said to cover her movement. "And, uh, how many bridesmaids are you planning on?"

She took herself back to her desk, rounding the corner and thanking the Gods that there was a solid piece of wood between the two of them now. What the hell was wrong with her?

"Just the one," Nic said, coming back to sit down.

"Just one?" Klara said, surprised. She'd expect at least three or four for a wedding like this.

Nic shrugged. "Don't know many women," she said. "At least as friends."

Klara's eyes narrowed. She definitely caught the undertone there, but it almost certainly meant nothing. She was reading something into nothing. Nic just meant that she didn't make female friends easily. Which, now that she thought about it, explained a whole lot.

"I'm sure that's not true," Klara said smoothly.

"Yes, it is," grinned Nic. She didn't seem to mind the fact that she had only one girl-friend.

"Psh," Klara said. "You're funny and pretty and women probably get intimidated, that's all."

"Funny and pretty, huh?"

Nic's dark eyes stared into hers for a fraction of a second too long. Twice now Nic had brushed up against her, once she'd put a hand on her elbow when they were looking at invitation samples, and every single time there was an opportunity she'd leaned over and gotten as close as she could get without touching Klara. And Klara was really starting to think that there was something here. Except that there wasn't.

Nic. Straight. Bride. Getting married. Get your head on straight.

The fact that Nic didn't have many female friends probably just meant that she wasn't great at judging boundaries when around other women, that's all. Nothing more than that.

"You'll make a beautiful bride," was all Klara said.

Her hand was lying on the desk and Nic's coffee cup was right next to it and Nic was reaching for the cup and for an instant their hands touched.

"Knock knock," shouted a voice.

Klara yanked her hand back. "In here."

"Greetings, ladies," George said, poking his head around the office door. "How's everything going?"

Klara couldn't even look him in the eye. She shuffled together some brochures on her desk. "Fine," she mumbled.

"It's going great," said Nic with more enthusiasm.

Klara glanced up just in time to catch the look that passed between the couple. A look that she didn't understand but that seemed almost irritated.

She took a deep breath. George being there had broken something in the room. Not necessarily in a bad way. "Can I get you a coffee?" she asked, polite and business-like.

"He's not stay—" began Nic.

"Absolutely," George said with a grin as he slid into the seat next to Nic's.

Klara didn't know that she could be both disappointed and relieved at the same time.

Chapter Eleven

She wasn't used to not getting what she wanted when it came to sex. That was the long and short of it. In life in general, sure. But when it came to women, she was confident enough and attractive enough that she was rarely told no. She'd never say so out loud, but in her head, Nic knew it was true. Which was why she was having such a problem being around Klara.

One appointment in her office and suddenly she was longing after the woman. Forbidden fruit, that's what it was. She shouldn't touch so the only thing she wanted to do was touch. Purely physical. Well, mostly physical. It had surprised her how quickly time had gone at the appointment.

"White or blue?" George said, hanging out of his bedroom door with a shirt in each hand.

"Uh, white."

He disappeared again, leaving the door open. She'd yelled at him after the wedding appointment, said that he didn't trust her, was checking up on her. It had taken a minute before she'd realized that time had just gone faster than she'd thought and he was there to pick her up as arranged. She'd apologized, but still felt shitty for jumping down his throat.

"Where you headed?" she asked. She shifted position, propped her legs up on the back of the couch so that she was more comfortable.

"Just to Tobias's place."

"Tobias? Again?" That made six dates that she could think of.

"Don't wait up," he called out in a sing-song voice.

"Wasn't planning on it." She paused, then asked: "Getting serious, is it?"

George came out of his bedroom and perched on the coffee table. "No. Yes. Maybe. I don't know."

He was actually blushing and Nic grinned. "I'll take that as a yes then?"

"He's, uh, he's pretty amazing," said George. "We'll have drinks sometime. Maybe next weekend. You can meet him. He's funny, God, I could listen to him talk for hours."

"Yeah, right, I'm sure that's exactly what you do," she said teasingly.

"No, really. Okay, there's plenty of the other too. But we talk. Really talk. Like he tells me about his life, what he thinks of things, we discuss things. It's… different. But nice. Like he cares about what's inside my head not just my body."

Nic smiled more gently. "He sounds lovely."

"He is lovely. And he's not married or otherwise dating, he's single and is looking only for a relationship, not for one-night stands, he's financially stable, he doesn't live with his parents, I could go on. But you get the picture."

"So it really is getting serious."

George looked at her, his blue eyes big and sparkling. "I think it might be."

"Good." She packed away her feelings about George being involved with someone. This wasn't her business. Their plan was their plan, and George was free to be with whomever he wanted. "You deserve a nice guy."

"Just as much as you deserve a nice girl."

Nic blew out a puff of air. "Speaking of which."

"Klara," supplied George.

"Klara," she agreed.

"I told you this was a bad idea," George said. "And it is. She's attractive, you're attracted, but she's our wedding planner. You'd be insane, Nic. Come on, you have to agree that Klara is off limits."

"I guess."

"And you say that like you're not convinced I'm right."

"I know you're right in my head," Nic said. "But my body isn't so sure."

George rolled his eyes. "Listen, you need to think things through here. Remember what's at stake. She could out you, this whole plan could come crashing down on our heads. Your whole plan."

"I just—"

"No, Nic. No 'justs'. She's the wedding planner. Apart from anything else, she thinks you're a straight woman about to get married to an amazingly handsome man. Me," he added with a lascivious wink. "So she's not going to sleep with you anyway."

"She might," Nic said, feeling like she was being challenged and knowing that she wasn't supposed to hear it that way.

"Nic..."

She sighed. Think of the consequences. Right. People told her that all the time. George and Sally specifically told her that all the time. The problem was that in her experience there wasn't always time to think about the consequences. When she was packing her bags to leave home she hadn't been thinking about the consequences. She'd just been thinking that she needed to leave. Now.

Besides, thinking about the consequences wasn't *fun*.

"Think about the money," George said. "Think about your end goal. Getting the trust fund."

Okay, that made more sense. She could do that. Probably.

"Think about us living a life of luxury. Well, not too much luxury, but at least not worrying about where the next meal's coming from."

"Right."

"Me in LA, you in Paris, come on, Nic. You know you want this."

"I do," she admitted.

"Then keep your eyes on the prize."

"Right," she said again.

He moved so that he was sitting on the couch next to her. "You know, we can still call all this off. We don't have to do it. We've never had to do it. I won't be mad or anything if you decide that this is crazy. It is crazy."

She took a deep breath then shook her head. "No, I'm being an idiot. Klara's hot, but one night of fun isn't worth sabotaging our whole plan for. You're right." Probably. He was probably right. "Besides, I'm looking forward to spending major holidays with your parents."

"Liar."

She grinned. "No, it'll be fun." Thanksgiving and Christmas with George's family for a few years. She could do that. It was more than worth the price. "And after that will come my absolute favorite part. Something I'm really looking forward to."

"Which is?"

"Telling your mother we're getting divorced."

George swatted her leg. "Lay off my mom. She's not as bad as you make her out to be."

"Your mom hates me."

"Jesus, she doesn't. How many times do I have to tell you?"

Nic stuck her tongue out and George started to tickle her feet and she was getting breathless and hysterical.

"Stop! Stop!"

His fingers stopped moving. "I'm only stopping because I don't want to be late for my date."

"Get the hell out of here!"

She was still giggling slightly as he closed the door behind him.

Another boring night in alone. She didn't exactly have the cash to throw around on going out. Not tonight. The apartment was empty and quiet and... if she narrowed her eyes she could see Klara leaning against the doorframe to her bedroom, beckoning her.

Her pulse quickened and a wave of warmth descended.

Klara.

God, she wanted to run her fingers through that blonde hair, tangle her fingers in it, pull Klara in roughly, kiss her, take her breath away.

Abruptly, she sat up. Enough. George was right, Klara was too risky.

Eyes on the prize.

Paris.

The idea was still a fairly new one. But it fit. Cooking was the one thing that she loved to do. Learning to do it professionally was an obvious next step. And Paris, well, who wouldn't want to live in Paris? Who wouldn't want a brand new start in a brand new city in a brand new country?

Nic didn't talk about it. Rarely thought about it, to be honest. But her life hadn't had the best start. And the thought that she could rise from nothingness to be the kind of girl that lived in Paris… It gave her hope. Something that she hadn't had for a long time. Hope that things could change. That she wouldn't always be scrabbling for rent and food and love.

Because love was in the picture too. It had taken a long time to get there. George and Sally had helped. And slowly she was beginning to realize that maybe there was someone inside her worthy of being loved, or at least liked.

And who knew? Paris was the city of lovers. Maybe when she finally had her shit together, maybe when she had a little money in the bank, some real qualifications, a real plan for her life. Maybe then there'd be room for something else, for someone else.

The idea was simultaneously exciting and terrifying.

Could she really ever trust anyone completely enough to let them in? Could she really love someone? She liked plenty of people. She lusted after many people. But loving, that was different, wasn't it?

How did it feel, she wondered. How would she know?

Big plans. So many big plans. Scarily big plans.

She reached for the TV remote and lay back on the couch. Big plans that she could do nothing about right now. So it was another night with reality TV. She flicked through the channels trying to ignore the shadowy picture of Klara standing in her bedroom doorway.

She was making smart decisions from now on.

And she was damn well going to think about the consequences of what she did. Even if life was more boring that way.

Chapter Twelve

The exhibition hall was buzzing and Klara grinned to herself. Wedding events were always well attended, and in general the guests were happy people, people that wanted to be there. Maybe that was why she'd always surrounded herself with weddings. It was tough to be depressed when everyone was talking about happy futures.

She skirted a stand with a display of silk flowers and finally spotted Jet at their assigned meeting place. She waved like a maniac until Jet saw her and bounded over.

"Already got my stuff done," Jet said, showing off a tote bag with a camera company's logo on it. "Plenty of promo materials and a couple of lenses I've been looking at getting. What are you in the market for?"

Klara grimaced. "Upmarket," she said. "And downmarket."

"Narrows things down a bit," Jet said, taking her arm and starting to propel her through the crowds. "I'm guessing upmarket is for the Gainer wedding?"

"Yep, I definitely need to expand my selection of samples. We're looking for invites and save the dates especially, and if a nice florist catches your eye, give me a shout. I could use a couple of new contacts, especially up-town ones."

"Got it," Jet said.

Arm in arm they strolled around the hall. It was nice to be with Jet, comfortable.

"Thanks for coming with me, you didn't have to."

"And miss all the thrilling excitement of a wedding show?" Jet said. She grinned. "Anyway, it's the least I could do. Well, I'm saying that assuming that you're going to let me photograph the Gainer wedding?"

"Absolutely," said Klara.

For a second she could see Nic standing in front of her, wavy black hair stirring in the breeze, leather jacket over a tight, white t-shirt.

"How's it going with the hot bride then?" Jet asked, as though she was some kind of mind-reader.

"Fine."

Jet stopped. "Uh-huh. That sounded good. Almost convincing."

But Klara was pulling away, avoiding the issue by picking up invitation samples. She heard a sigh behind her but knew that if she was quiet long enough Jet would get the picture and change the subject.

If there was one thing she didn't want to talk about it was Nic Salinas. If only because she was confused. She could have sworn that the woman was flirting with her. God knows, she flirted enough herself that she knew how these things worked. But Nic couldn't have been. Shouldn't have been. And then George had arrived and... the air in the room had changed. And now she was confused and turned on and disappointed in herself and... and she really didn't know how to even talk about the way she was feeling.

"What about downmarket?" Jet said, sidling up to her.

"Huh?"

"You said you were looking for upmarket stuff for the Gainer wedding and downmarket. Why downmarket?"

"Ah," said Klara. It had been a small brain-wave, but every little bit helped. Maybe this was going to be her sweet spot, the thing that made her name in the wedding market. "Well, I've been thinking."

"Always dangerous."

"Haha. One of the worst parts of being a planner are all the couples that come to my office and then don't book my services."

"Because they're just looking for ideas of yours to steal that they can implement themselves," Jet said with a sour look.

"No! Because they can't afford to use a wedding planner."

Jet shook her head but smiled. "You always look on the bright side, don't you? Always look for the best in people."

"I try," Klara said stoutly. "So, my idea is that I put together some wedding packages for low budget weddings. Small venues, discount vendors, that sort of thing. Get the prices down as much as I can. That way there'll be something for everyone. Profits will be slim, but hopefully I'll be able to make up for that in volume."

"Makes sense, I guess," said Jet. "It's hardly the ideal market."

"I don't care. Someone needs to take care of people that want a lovely wedding at a low cost. I want to make people happy!"

"I get it, I get it," Jet said. "Alright, why not? It's not going to cost you anything to try. Maybe you're right, maybe there's a gap in the market and you're going to fill it."

"I need something to get people through the doors," she began. But she was cut off by the sound of her mobile ringing.

She stepped aside. "Hello?"

"Hi, Klara?"

Even the voice made her heart pound. She took a deep breath. "Yes. Hi, Nic."

"I was just wondering if we could firm up the appointment for dress shopping?"

For a brief second Klara had a flash of a vision. Nic in her underwear, pulling on a wedding dress. Something strange happened inside her. She was suddenly far too hot. She closed her eyes but that only made the vision stronger. She cleared her throat. "Yes, of course."

"LET ME guess," Jet said when the phone conversation was over. "Hot bride?"

There was no point in denying it. Klara nodded.

"You flushed like a damn beacon, girl. You've got it bad. Are you sure you know what you're doing here?"

"I, uh, well, no. Not really."

Jet stared at her.

"I don't. Maybe this was all a really bad idea," Klara said. "But it's not like I have much choice. My entire business is now depending on me getting this wedding done. If I don't get paid for this one then I won't be paying rent next month."

A hand reached out and patted her shoulder. "I'd help if I could."

"I know. But you can't. This wedding can. So I'll suck it up and..."

"And be love-lorn and horny for the next however many weeks until the wedding."

"Four weeks," Klara said. "That's one of the saving graces of all this. For whatever reason they're on a short time schedule. They want this wedding like yesterday."

"Maybe she's pregnant," Jet said as she took Klara's arm again.

"She's not."

"Wishful thinking?"

Klara opened her mouth to reply then shut it again, reconsidering. If she couldn't be honest with Jet, then who could she be honest with?

"Maybe," she allowed. "Maybe my judgment's getting all screwed up."

"Meaning what?" asked Jet as she steered them toward a stand offering wine samples.

"Meaning that I could have sworn she was flirting with me the other day in my office. I know that sounds crazy. But she kept getting close to me, almost touching me, brushing my arm. All the things you do to show someone you're interested without actually just coming right out and saying that you're interested."

"That does sound crazy," Jet agreed, picking up two wine samples and handing one to Klara.

"Right? But I don't know. There's something not right about all of this. I can't put my finger on it. There's something different here. I see a lot of weddings and a lot of couples and this... I don't know."

"It's not impossible that she was flirting with you," Jet said, downing her wine in one shot and looking hopefully at the vendor on the off-chance that she'd get another.

"She's straight and about to get married, Jet."

"You don't know that," said Jet, giving up on the vendor and moving on. "Well, you know she's getting married. But maybe she's bi."

"Still doesn't overcome the 'she's about to get married' obstacle."

"Maybe she's trying to get something out of her system," Jet said. "Maybe she and her intended have an open relationship."

"Okay. You're not exactly helping clear up my confusion here."

"I'm just saying that it's not unthinkable that she's interested too. I mean, if you want to sleep with the woman then, well, it could be possible."

Klara sighed. "I'm not a one-night stand kind of person."

"I know, you're a falling in love at the literal drop of a hat kind of person," Jet said. "But that doesn't mean you can't change."

For a tempting second she thought about the way Nic's hand felt on hers. And then she shook herself. No. No way. No how. She wasn't that kind of person. Besides, she wasn't about to risk the future of her business on making a pass at someone who almost certainly wasn't interested, no matter what Jet said.

"Come on," she said. "There's a huge paper vendor over there. I want to check out what they have."

Jet held back for a second, then grumbled. "Fine," she said, accepting that the conversation was over.

Now if only Klara could forget everything that had been said. If only she could extinguish the little flame of hope that Jet had lit when she said Nic might be interested. If only she hadn't had to take on this damn wedding at all.

Chapter Thirteen

Nic had the world divided into two types of women. Those that felt comfortable in a dress, and those that didn't. She was firmly in the second camp. Her regular uniform consisted of jeans and a shirt of some kind, though she could be persuaded into shorts when the weather got hot. It wasn't that she'd never worn a dress. Obviously she had. First communion, for example. It just seemed like every time she put a dress on she ended up creating less than stellar memories.

But complain as she might, George had absolutely drawn the line at getting married in jeans.

"You want this to look real?" he'd said. "Then you need to do it right. You think I want to be strangled by a tie and cummerbund all day?"

"Not the same thing," she'd grumbled. "At least you won't have a draft blowing around your hoo-ha."

He'd grinned an evil grin. "And here was I thinking that you enjoyed things blowing around down there."

She'd thrown a cushion at him and the argument had eventually ended only because she knew that he was right. She needed to suck things up. That didn't make things any easier though. She was bizarrely nervous as she walked down the street, nearing the address that Klara had given her.

She pushed open a door, a tiny bell tinkling, and stepped inside a snowball. Honestly, you'd think that people would get more creative with weddings, but no, it seemed like white was still the order of the day. A motherly older lady smiled from behind a counter and Nic was just about to greet her when Klara appeared from behind a curtain.

"Nic, you made it."

She was smiling but Nic was swallowing down a groan. In all her worrying about trying on stupid dresses she'd conveniently forgotten that this would mean spending the entire afternoon with Klara. An afternoon that, thanks to tradition, wasn't going to be interrupted by George. There was a stirring in her stomach. Klara was dressed in a black skirt and white shirt, very professional, but oddly naughty as well. Like a teacher, one that Nic suddenly wanted to bend over one of the chairs in the waiting area.

"Nic?"

She jumped to attention. "Uh, yeah, sorry, just, um... Just a little overwhelmed by..." She gestured around at all the dresses.

"There's nothing to worry about," said the older woman, stepping around her counter. "I've set up a selection of different styles in the fitting lounge, and Klara will lead you through everything. All you need to do is choose something." She turned to Klara. "Just let me know if you ladies need any help."

Klara smiled gratefully and moved to Nic. Nic felt her elbow being clasped by a warm hand as Klara steered her back into the room behind the shop. She felt like she was being escorted to her bed chamber, and her stomach did another flip.

"We've got everything we need in here," Klara said. "Dresses to try on, comfortable couches to sit on, and, of course, champagne." She grinned and passed Nic a glass. "Drink up."

Nic did as she was ordered, draining the glass in one and handing it back. When she saw the look on Klara's face, she realized that she'd done the wrong thing. "Um, nerves?" she offered.

Klara laughed. "There's no need to be nervous at all. This is supposed to be fun."

"Not really my idea of fun," Nic admitted.

"I get it," Klara said sympathetically. "Dresses aren't really your thing, right?"

Nic shook her head feeling young and dumb in a way that she rarely felt these days.

"Why don't we just try one on and see how you feel?" Klara asked. "We can go from there. If you truly hate it then you can opt for a pants-suit. It's not the traditional choice, but..."

She let the sentence hang there and Nic was beginning to hate the word traditional. But then she was captured by the shining blue of Klara's eyes, by the dimple in her cheek as she smiled and the thought of touching that soft skin and she nodded and allowed Klara to lay a dress over her arms and gently push her into the cabin.

Automatically, Nic began unbuttoning her jeans, pulling up her shirt.

"So, how did you and George meet?" Klara asked from the other side of the curtain.

"Um, we've been friends for a while," Nic said, concentrating on lifting up her t-shirt.

"Oh?"

And something in the tone told her that this wasn't the answer that Klara was looking for. "I mean, we were friends first," she qualified. "Then um, things progressed?" It came out as a question.

"That's nice," Klara said. "It's important to be friends. A lot of couples don't get that."

Nic was sliding down her jeans, feeling more naked than ever and suddenly she was in her underwear and it occurred to her that Klara was within touching distance. That just on the other side of the curtain she was there. She gulped and felt her pulse quicken. Her arm brushed against her chest as she reached for the dress on its hanger and her nipple stiffened inside her bra.

Jesus Christ.

She fought through the fluffy material of the dress, eventually managing to get it over her head but then found that she couldn't fasten the thing.

"Help?"

"Coming," Klara said, drawing back the curtain. "Turn around."

Nic obediently turned and then she felt cool fingers on her skin as Klara fiddled with the fastenings and zipped her up. It was enough to make her gasp, a sound that was hidden by the hiss of the zipper.

"Well, what do you think?" Klara asked.

AS NIC TURNED KLARA had to bite her tongue to stop from crying out.

The dress was slim, skimming over curves that she hadn't known Nic had. The startling white of the fabric stood out against the creamy brown of Nic's skin. Curling, dark hair fell over bare shoulders that Klara had an urge to litter with kisses. She felt a burning of desire deep in her stomach. Shit. This wasn't good.

"Is it that terrible?"

She blinked back to attention to see Nic's face was concerned. "No," she said quickly. "No, not at all. Just, maybe the train isn't really you?" The fluffy material at the bottom of the dress gathered around Nic's ankles.

Nic gazed downward then shrugged. "Alrighty then. Let's try another." She turned around. "Undress me."

Klara's heart sped up to the point that she was sure it was audible. Her hands started to shake. It took a second for the real meaning of the words to sink in. Then she reached for the zipper. Undress me. She slid the zip down. Undress me. And carefully, slowly backed away, not trusting herself to do or say anything more.

"Thanks," Nic said, going back behind the curtain.

Three more dresses. Three more times she faced the soft, tanned skin of Nic's back as she pulled zippers up and down. Three more times her hands shook. Three more times she wanted nothing more than to grab that waist from behind, to let her hands wander down over those rounded hips, to press herself up against Nic, to drink in her scent and feel her skin. And three more times she backed the hell off, cursing her hormones and horniness and swearing that she was going out that very night to get laid and break whatever this spell was that Nic had over her.

It was the fourth dress that was the problem.

A line of tiny hooks curved down the spine of the dress and Nic was getting tired. She put her hands on the wall of the fitting cabin, leaning against it, pushing her butt out a little as Klara's aching, shaking fingers tried to hook each tiny piece of metal to its eye.

It took forever. Minute after minute, her fingers brushing against Nic's skin and her breathing getting faster and neither of them talking as she concentrated. And when she was done she tried to take a step back, forgetting that she was so close to the opposite wall and Nic spun around at the exact same time and then there she was, pinned back against the wall by Nic. Dark eyes so close she could fall into them, breath sweet and warm on her cheek, and it seemed so natural, so right, that her lips were parting before she could stop them, her hips were arching up before she could say no, her skin was tingling before she knew what was happening.

And then common sense kicked in and she was on the spur of making a decision, but it was too late. Far too late.

Nic was already there.

Those plump, pink lips were already a fraction of a centimeter from hers.

They were already touching.

And then, they were already kissing.

The wrongness disappeared, replaced by the sensation of soft lips, a tongue searching for her own, a warm body pushing her back against the wall and her own nerves shooting impulses to all the right places. She heard herself moan, pushing back, letting her hands touch that soft, long hair, wanting to tangle her fingers in it and drink Nic in, wanting more.

And then it stopped.

They both drew back.

She saw the look on Nic's face. Suddenly realized what they'd done. Reality kicked in. And then she couldn't look anymore. She pulled her gaze away, sick to her stomach at the thought of what this was, what had happened.

"I, uh, I'll go and get Mary up front to unhook you from the dress," she said quietly.

Her legs shook as she walked away and she could feel Nic's eyes on her and oh God, what had she done?

Chapter Fourteen

"I can't see the difference."

She was getting angry, her face prickling with heat and she didn't want to be. She liked being in control, liked being cool and calm and collected. But George had known from the second that she'd walked in the door that something was wrong, that something had happened.

"Really?" he said. "You don't see a difference? You want to think about that one for a hot minute?"

And what a thing to happen. That kiss.

She hadn't meant to, she truly hadn't. But turning around and seeing Klara right there, seeing her eyes so blue she could swim in them, seeing her lips part, she hadn't been in control then. Far from it. She'd jumped in with both feet and consequences be damned.

"I don't need to think about it," she said now. "You're dating Tobias. So I don't see why it's such a damn problem if I kiss Klara."

It wasn't like this was going to be a long term thing. In fact, it might not be anything. Klara had drawn back, a sick look on her face, and she'd hurried off and for the last twenty minutes of their appointment she hadn't come within spitting distance. And Nic hadn't known what to say to make things better, her head had still been swimming from that kiss and she'd wanted more. A lot more.

Then Klara had made her escape and she'd come home and George had seen her face and had known and now this. An argument that she didn't want, and one that she knew wasn't right. She didn't have a leg to stand on, no matter what she was saying.

"Kiss Klara?" George said, sitting upright on the sofa. "Kiss our wedding planner, you mean?"

"Yeah, so?"

"So?" said George. "You're doing it again, Nic. You're just disregarding everything else because of something you want. You don't think about the consequences, you don't think about anyone else, you just think about what you want in this one second. And life doesn't work that way. All this, all this talking and planning and scheming and you're willing to blow it all up for a kiss?"

For more than a kiss, she thought. Because she had to have more now. She knew that, knew that she wouldn't settle for anything less than Klara in her bed. Assuming, of course, that she could persuade her.

"I'm not going to get caught," she said. "In the same way that you'd better not get caught, swanning around town with your new boyfriend."

"For fuck's sake, Nic. Have someone else, anyone you like, but leave Klara alone!"

"No!"

"Then why are we doing this?" he said. "Why bother? I mean, it's not like anyone's forcing you to. If you want to elope with the wedding planner then go right ahead. But why are you putting me, and my family through this?"

"Because—"

"Because of the money!" He was shouting now. "Is that what all of this is? Because that sounds an awful lot like you're using me, Nic, and I don't like that."

"No, I'm not! George—"

"Then take a second to think and keep your damned pants on!" he yelled.

There was a thumping as the downstairs neighbor banged on the ceiling with a broom. Too much noise. Thin ceilings, a cheap apartment, and too much noise.

"Georgie, come on, we can make this work. I can make this work."

But he was mad now and there was no stopping it. She knew him well enough to know that he would get more and more angry the longer she tried to talk him out of it. She grabbed her jacket from the back of the armchair that she'd dropped it on.

"You need to promise me that you won't do this," he said. "Or promise me that you'll change the damn wedding planner, or whatever it takes, Nic. I'm not inviting disaster into my life like this."

She was already leaving though, the door banging behind her so that the downstairs neighbor yelled again.

SHE WAS early, but so was Sally so it didn't matter.

"You've got a face like a smacked arse," Sally said, sitting down at the window-side table.

"And you watch far more BBC America than is good for you," responded Nic.

Sally rolled her eyes. "And here's me inviting you out for a drink to apologize for missing your wedding dress fitting. If you're going to be in a mood all night then this is going to be a very long evening."

Nic smiled at this. Smiled because Sally hadn't said she'd leave, had just assumed that no matter what kind of mood Nic was in that they'd drink together. It was nice to have someone that could always be counted on.

"Gonna tell me what happened?" Sally said as she waved a waiter over. "I'll take a vodka and tonic."

"Make that two," Nic said. "Had an argument with George."

"I thought the arguments came after you got married," Sally said. Then seeing that Nic was in no mood for joking, she added: "What did you guys argue about?"

"I kissed Klara." No point beating around the bush.

"Jesus, Nic."

"Don't you start," Nic said. "He's mad as hell and is demanding that I drop Klara."

"No fear," Sally said. Drinks had arrived and she picked hers up and clinked her glass against Nic's. "I learned a long time ago that telling you not to do something is a mistake. One I won't be repeating."

"Jeez, I slid down the stair-rail of your building one time."

"And I spent the rest of the evening in the ER with you and your concussion," Sally reminded her. "However, I will say that George might have a point about this not being incredibly smart."

Nic shrugged. "I didn't mean to do it. Honestly, I didn't. She's just... I don't know. There's something about her. I want to get to know her more."

Sally smirked. "Right. And we all know what 'get to know her' is code for."

"I'm serious!" Then Nic laughed. "Alright, alright. I want to sleep with her. But what's so wrong with that? We're both adults. George isn't actually going to be my husband, and anyway he's got this new guy he's seeing. I'm not planning on getting caught in flagrante by his mother or anything. I can keep a secret."

Sally narrowed her eyes. "Can you? And what about this Klara? Is she interested?"

"I—" She stopped herself. Was Klara interested? "Maybe. She kissed me back."

And she looked. She looked when she thought Nic wouldn't notice. She stood a millimeter too close. There was something there, she'd swear to it.

"Well, as of now, that poor woman thinks that she's kissed a straight girl mere weeks before her wedding. Which I would guess means she's freaking out."

Nic blew out a breath. She hadn't thought about that. First George was mad at her, now Klara was weirded out by her, Sally might be the one person she knew that currently liked her and would speak with her.

"I suppose I should explain things."

"If you're going to pursue things you should."

Nic was silent for a while. Was she going to pursue things? She wasn't an idiot, she could see the danger here. But she was careful, she was a grown up, there was no real reason she couldn't have her cake and eat it too.

"You should probably talk things through with George as well," Sally said. "He could cancel this whole wedding escapade if he chose to."

Nic nodded. "He thinks I'm doing it for the money," she said. It had hurt when he'd said that. Stung.

"And you're not?"

Nic sighed. "The money should be his. Whether he's gay or straight shouldn't matter. I could see when he told me about it that he'd already dismissed the trust fund, that he'd already decided that he would never get the money that was gifted to him just because he wasn't about to marry a woman. And I hated that."

"Hated to see someone treated unfairly?" Sally asked. "Or did you hate it because you don't want to see gay people treated differently? Because it reminded you in a way of what your family did to you?"

Nic groaned. "I hate it when you do that."

"What?"

"Therapize me."

"You deserve it," said Sally. "And George deserves to know the truth about why you're doing this. You should be honest with him, explain to him. Don't let him think that you're doing this just for the cash. That's a disservice to yourself. It's unfair to you."

Nic nodded. Sally was right. She lifted her glass. "You know, it's been a hell of a day," she said. "Do you think we could drink now?"

Sally grinned. "Absolutely. Now who am I drinking to? The blushing bride or the wedding planner?"

Nic said nothing. She tipped her glass against Sally's, then drank nearly half the contents in one gulp. She closed her eyes against the sting of the alcohol and immediately saw Klara, felt her lips, felt her warmth. Jesus, she had it bad.

Chapter Fifteen

Fluffy pajamas: check. Wine: check. Snacks: check. Best friend? The doorbell rang and Klara jumped for it.

"Thank God you're here," she said as Jet strode in.

"Well, you did say it was an emergency." Jet looked her up and down, taking in the entire effect, then grimaced. "Is it that bad? Like Mickey Mouse pajama pants kind of bad?"

Klara nodded.

She was trying to be light about this, trying to be just the ditzy blonde that got herself into trouble. Trying so hard. But she should have known that Jet wouldn't be taken in by things, that she'd have to let out some of the emotions inside.

"Someone die?" Jet asked.

Klara shook her head.

"Um, break in? Bankruptcy? Oh, embezzlement?"

"Who'd embezzle from me?" Klara asked. "I work for myself." But she knew that Jet was playing along.

Jet shed her jacket, kicked off her boots and picked up the wine bottle. "Well then, I'm guessing this has to do with affairs of the heart and given that, I'm also guessing that this has to do with the bride. Am I right?"

Klara nodded again as Jet popped the cork out of the bottle and glugged wine into two glasses.

"Is it as bad as I'm thinking?" Jet asked.

"Worse."

"How much worse?"

Jet passed her a wine glass and Klara sunk to the floor with it cradled in her hands. "We kissed," she said in a voice so small she wondered if Jet could hear her.

There was a long silence as Jet sipped thoughtfully at her wine. When she finally spoke, she was cool, logical, not at all emotional or judgmental. "Did you kiss her or did she kiss you?"

"I kissed her," Klara said immediately.

But it didn't sound right. In her memory that wasn't what had happened at all. In her mind, Nic had been the one to lean in, the one to press her up against the wall, the one to disappear her into the kiss. But that couldn't possibly be right, could it? She must be mistaken. She must have lost her head for a second, been drunk on the closeness of Nic, crossed the line.

"Are you sure about that?" Jet asked.

"Yes." A pause. "No."

"So, it was a real kiss? Regardless of who started it? You both kissed each other?"

Klara nodded even though she couldn't quite believe it herself.

"And then?"

"And then I realized what was happening and I walked away and behaved like a professional," Klara said. A professional with shaking legs and sweating hands, a professional that had longed to flee but hadn't been able to bring herself to break the appointment.

Jet sucked air through her teeth. "And now?"

Which was the real question, wasn't it? Not that she needed Jet to tell her what to do. But she did need a real person to hear her words, a real person to confirm what she already knew.

"Now I need to pull out of the wedding, don't I?"

She hadn't meant to add the tag on the end of the question. Deep inside she knew that she was hoping that Jet had a different answer, that she'd somehow think of a way that she could keep the wedding and kiss the bride. And maybe kiss her again, said a little voice in the back of her head that she promptly dismissed.

This time Jet blew a breath out. "Probably," she allowed. She turned her eyes to Klara. "Can you afford to do that?"

"Can I afford not to do that?" Klara said. "I don't know what's going on here, Jet. I like her, I really do. And I know that I say that all the time, but it's true all the time. I really do like her and I think that maybe, somehow, she might even like me back. But that doesn't matter, does it? What matters is that this is my job and I'm supposed to be helping her plan her wedding and if I can't do that, if I can't keep my feelings to myself, then I have no business being involved."

There. She'd said it.

"And the money?" Jet pressed.

She shrugged. "I need it. Of course I do. I could try and get some kind of loan though, that's what I was thinking. Just until I get some of the budget wedding packages put together. Kind of like an investment, but from the bank."

"You definitely can't put up with this for another, what, three weeks?"

"Jet..."

"Alright," said Jet, shrugging. "Then yes, you have to quit. As much as I'm all for you finding Ms. Right, this particular Ms. Right is about to become Mrs. Right. You need to back off if you can't control your feelings around her. And that means quitting the wedding."

Klara felt her heartbeat speed up. She knew Jet was right, she knew that she had to pull out of the wedding. But the thought of not seeing Nic again. The thought of never again experiencing a kiss like that...

She hadn't been completely truthful. She did like women all the time. She did really like Nic. But there was something different here, something she couldn't put her finger on. That kiss had been like sliding into a warm bath, like putting on a pair of hand-made shoes, like coming home. Nothing in her life had even felt that right. Like Cinderella's slipper.

"Klara?"

She took a deep breath then she nodded. "I'll call them tomorrow. It's the right thing to do."

"And you always do the right thing," Jet said, studying her. "We all know that."

Just for once, Klara wished that Jet didn't know her quite that well.

SHE WAS procrastinating, putting off the moment when she made the call. She knew that. Whether it was because she didn't want to end things or because she couldn't handle hearing Nic's voice on the line, she didn't know. But she was definitely procrastinating.

At least she was being productive though. A half dozen tabs were open on her computer, each outlining the terms of a business loan with a different bank. All had their requirements and she was getting a gnawing of doubt in her stomach. Was a loan the right thing to do? All that money and no guarantee that she could pay it off in the end. And no guarantee that she'd get the loan in the first place either.

It felt like cutting the strings of her parachute in the hopes that some other sky-diver was going to scoop her out of the sky. Which was yet another reason not to make the call.

If she closed her eyes she could be right back there. She could be pressed against that wall, Nic flush against her, their hearts beating in sync, their lips meeting for the first time. She could smell the scent of Nic's shampoo, could feel her hair between her fingers, could taste her.

Would that memory ever go away? Would it fade with time? She didn't know whether she wanted it to or not.

Wouldn't it be just her luck? To search the world for her Princess Charming and have her finally be unobtainable. Fairytale Princes never had this problem. There'd be some traumatizing Disney films if they did.

The phone rang and she considered not answering it. She was building up her courage now. She had to get this done and... And her hand was already picking up the receiver, already ready for more procrastination. Anything to avoid telling Nic that she was done.

"Sorensson Wedding Designs."

"Klara, hi, it's Nic."

The silence went on for what felt like hours but could only have been a second or two. Her pulse raced at the sound of Nic's voice and her stomach twisted because now she couldn't procrastinate anymore, could she? She cleared her voice and swallowed before she responded.

"Hi."

Yeah, way to communicate. The word hung in the air and the line crackled and her arm shook with the desire to slam the phone down to give this more thought to come to some kind of different decision.

"I, uh, I was hoping that you might meet with me tomorrow. I think we need to talk."

That was an understatement. At least they were on the same page. But a meeting? Really? Was that safe? Klara's heart hammered and her mouth was dry. She should do this now, over the phone, there was no need to meet.

"Yes, of course." Her mouth betrayed her, letting her heart speak before her brain could catch up with what was happening.

There was a sigh on the other end of the phone, relief she thought, though she couldn't be sure. "Great. There's a café on the corner of fifth street, do you know it? I could meet you there after my shift. Say, around six?"

"I'll be there," Klara said before she could screw things up any further. She put the phone down gently.

So there it was. She'd get to see Nic one more time. The only question was which of them would get in first. Would she be fired before she could quit? But she was too busy thinking about seeing Nic again to force herself to care.

Chapter Sixteen

She was struggling to pull her jeans on over socks that were far too thick. And George was leaning against the bedroom door.

"So you're doing all this for me?" he said.

He'd calmed down now, as she'd known he would once left alone. "Yes," she said, finally getting one leg of her jeans on. "I'm not gonna lie to you, Georgie. Obviously, getting some cash will help me out too." Paris, she thought in her head and a little thrill ran down her spine. "But I'd do it for nothing, swear to God."

He sighed. "You know, I'd practically forgotten about the trust fund. I knew that I was never going to get it, so..."

"Exactly my point," she said, standing up having achieved her objective. Putting the socks on first had been stupid. "And this way we both get something out of it. So maybe you're right, I am doing this for the money, but I'm doing it for *your* money."

"Fair enough," George said. "But the issue still stands—"

She fixed her shirt and interrupted. "Yep, it does. I'm playing with fire, I got it. But I also get that it's not your business, George. I don't tell you who to date and you don't tell me."

"I worry."

"I know you do. But I'm an adult, Klara and I are both adults. I can handle this. And it's probably nothing. There's all kinds of outcomes here. Maybe she quits and we hire another planner, maybe I fire her because she sucks in bed, maybe we live a happy undercover life with me as your wife and Klara as your... secretary. I don't know. I do know that happiness is rare and you grab it when you find it."

He tapped his fingers on the door then nodded. "Alright, this is your decision. But I want it on the record that I'm not happy with it."

"Fine," Nic said, grinning at him. "I don't need you to be happy with it. But I also don't want to keep things from you. You're my friend above all else, Georgie, and this wedding shouldn't get in the way. It should bring us closer together."

She did a little twirl and he nodded appreciatively. "Looking good."

"Thank you, almost-husband. And as you'd say, don't wait up."

She moved to leave the room but George was still standing in front of the door. She paused in front of him, wondering for a second if he was really going to move. Then he sighed again and scooted away, letting her slide past.

"Be careful, Nic," was all he said.

"Always am."

SHE LOVED this part. The undecided part where anything and everything could happen. The part where Klara might slap her or might fall into her arms. The part where her heart hammered and she had no idea where things were going but she had hope.

The café was quiet and she arrived a little early, choosing a corner seat and ordering two lattes. She didn't want a waitress interrupting what she wanted to say. Or maybe she didn't want anyone overhearing. And she was casually studying her phone when Klara walked in.

The hairs on the back of her neck prickled but she didn't look up, didn't want to seem over-eager even though she ached to see her. Only when Klara's shadow inched over the table did she finally tear her eyes away from her phone.

And there she was. Blonde bangs touching her eyelashes, wide mouth worried and eyes large and blue. Given her choice, she'd throw Klara down on the table and take her right here. Which was the issue that most pressingly needed taking care of. Well, the second issue. Klara deserved some explanations first.

"Hi."

"Hi." Klara sat.

"I, uh, already ordered coffees."

"Okay."

Klara's eyes darted to either side and she was obviously nervous and Nic felt sorry for her. She was about to jump in when Klara spoke instead.

"I think it's only fair to be up-front. I'll be quitting the wedding."

Klara looked at her hesitantly, expecting a reaction, but Nic didn't give her one. Instead she watched the waitress bring their coffees and thanked her politely and added sugar and stirred all before turning her attention back to Klara.

Was she being cruel? Maybe. It wasn't intentional. Having Klara sitting here addled her brain, made her forget her carefully prepared speech. She needed a moment to collect herself. She took a deep breath.

"Before you do that, and I'm not saying you can't quit, there's something that you really need to know."

"Ms. Salinas, there's really nothing that you could tell me—"

Nic didn't miss that Klara had reverted to her formal name. "No, listen first."

Klara closed her mouth, bit her lip, but nodded.

"George and I aren't really getting married. Well, we are, but we aren't."

A slow frown spread across Klara's face, confusion growing in her eyes. Nic sighed and then gently began to explain to Klara exactly what was going on. Klara's eyes widened further and further as she got to the truth.

"So it's all fake?"

Nic shrugged. "Mostly."

"I, uh, don't know what to say."

"Then don't say anything," Nic said. Klara's hand was on the table and she moved hers closer so that they were almost touching. "Because there's something else we need to discuss, isn't there?"

Klara blushed and Nic's stomach flipped and she moaned under her breath. And when Klara nodded she almost kissed her right there. But she held herself back.

"We kissed," Nic said, lowering her voice. "We kissed and, correct me if I'm wrong, but it was amazing. Wasn't it?"

The tiniest of nods.

"There's something here, Klara, an attraction. I want you, and I think you want me too. And I think we owe it to life to try things out, to keep hunting for our happiness until we find it, to do anything we can to find that connection, don't you?"

Another tiny nod and Klara's lips were parting and Nic couldn't deal with hearing the word no from her, couldn't deal with all the reasons why this was a bad idea, so she pre-empted them.

"I know this is a bad idea. I know it's dangerous and maybe we shouldn't. But I also know that I want you, Klara. So badly. And I'm willing to take the risk."

"Take the risk to do what?" Klara's voice was husky.

"To try this, to see what happens. Maybe this is all hormonal. Probably it is. We get it out of our systems and move on. Easy."

Her fingers were creeping toward Klara's now and at the first touch she felt a shot of warmth up her arm. Klara was opening her mouth again, but Nic jumped in.

"Don't you want me?"

Klara's mouth slammed shut again. Then she nodded. "But—"

"No buts," Nic said. "Take the risk. Let's do this. There's no point analyzing and talking about it if it's nothing but a roll in the hay, is there? Let's do what we want to do so badly and maybe then we can just go back to working on the wedding and it'll be fine. Or you can quit, or whatever you want."

She knew that she should put more thought into this. But having Klara right there, touching her, she just couldn't. All she could think about was Klara.

Klara who was pushing her chair back, standing up, walking away. Fuck.

Nic threw some money down on the table and ran out, chasing after her, catching her by the elbow. Klara turned to face her and Nic had no more words. She put her hand to the back of Klara's head and pulled her into a kiss so deep that it made the rest of the world disappear. For achingly long seconds she kept her eyes pressed closed, tasted Klara, smelled Klara, filled her senses with her. And then, finally, she came up for breath.

"Tell me you don't want this and I'll walk away, I promise."

Klara's cheeks were red, her breath was coming in gasps and Nic thought that if she moved her hand Klara might just fall over.

"It's a bad idea."

"I know," Nic agreed. "But can you live life not knowing what we'd be like together?"

"A very bad idea."

"Then tell me to go."

Klara looked down and for a moment Nic thought she was going to tell her to leave. The street was noisy, cars beeping, people shuffling past, and her heart sank and she was ready to walk away. Ready even though it was already starting to hurt just to think about. Then Klara looked up again.

"My apartment is this way," was all she said.

She turned and walked away and Nic had to run a step to keep up with her.

Chapter Seventeen

She walked with more confidence than she felt. If Nic was following then... good. If she wasn't, well, that was just what was supposed to happen. It was only two blocks to her apartment and she was determined not to turn around and check.

It was a culmination of many things. Jet telling her that she always did the right thing. Nic asking her if she could live not knowing what could happen between them. And her own libido, she had to factor that in too. She had to take into account the fact that Nic made her blood boil, made her stomach turn somersaults, made her mouth water.

Nic wasn't straight.

The news should have come as more of a surprise than it did. But hadn't she known all along that there was something off about this wedding? Hadn't she sensed something from the very beginning? And now she was right. And non-judgmental. Because it wasn't her job to judge how other people lived their lives.

Nic had been honest with her, she thought. Honest about her motivations, about the money. She'd been open about wanting her. Open about the possibility that this could all be nothing, that maybe it was just hormones and instant attraction and maybe it could lead nowhere.

All of this was why she was walking toward her apartment. All of it jumbled together in her head and making little sense except for the over-riding knowledge that she wanted Nic.

Whatever else was going to happen would happen.

Hell, she'd been going to quit the wedding anyway, right? So what difference did it make? At least this way she'd get laid in the process.

Or maybe, said that annoying voice in the back of her head, just maybe this was the one.

She shook her head to get rid of the thought and pulled out her keys and her door was coming up and still she hadn't checked. Maybe she wasn't there at all. Maybe no one was.

She put her keys into the lock, turned, pushed the door open. And she thought she felt a stirring of breeze as she walked through the door.

She walked toward the elevator, hitting the button. And now she was almost sure that there was a presence behind her. Not touching, not talking, just watching and breathing and a shiver went down her spine as the elevator dinged and the doors opened.

She stepped inside. And now she had no choice but to turn around. Still, she hesitated for a brief second, taking a deep breath before she turned.

Nic was already so close that they were practically touching.

She'd come.

Of course she had.

She could smell that shampoo, could smell leather, could smell coconut and lemon and something else, musky, deep, thrilling. Neither of them spoke. Neither of them moved. Until the elevator doors slid closed and then everything happened at the same time, every action mirrored until Klara was pushed back against the wall and Nic was there, her heat, her lips, her hands, and like an explosion Klara was wet and gasping for breath.

She tangled her hands into Nic's hair, pulling her in deeper, feeling her hips buck up to meet Nic's, the metal of Nic's belt buckle digging into her stomach. She tasted cinnamon and coffee and her pulse was racing and she never, ever wanted this to end.

But the elevator dinged insistently and Nic pulled back, eyes dark and hot and gleaming. She grinned. "Should I push the button for the penthouse? Give us a little more time in here?"

Klara gasped and laughed at the same time, still overwhelmed with sensations. "Better not," she said. "Maybe there's a security camera."

Nic nodded in serious agreement. "We've definitely given enough of a free show. They're gonna have to pay if they want to see any more than this."

There was going to be more than this. Klara's skin prickled with delight. She slid out from Nic's grasp, pulled her keys out again and staggered toward the door of her apartment. There was no doubt that she was being followed now, Nic's hand was on the small of her back as though she couldn't break contact.

Unlocking the door was a brief pause, a respite, an intermission. She did it slowly, the anticipation of what was going to happen next painful and exciting at the same time. Then the door was open and she was being pushed inside and then something else was happening.

Strong arms lifted her, Nic's foot kicked the door closed.

"Bedroom?" Nic whispered into her ear.

Klara nodded in the general direction and Nic carried her there, practically throwing her down on the bed. Klara laughed.

"Never been carried to bed before?" Nic asked.

"Never," she said.

And Nic was already there, next to her and then on top of her and the kisses continued and continued until Klara was ready to beg for more. And only later did she realize that Nic had been nervous. That strong, confident Nic had been stalling for time.

Instincts took over. She could take the teasing no more. She rolled, bringing Nic with her, until she was on top, her hands pulling at Nic's shirt, lifting it over her head and baring the sports bra underneath. Nic was watching her, eyes still dark with lust, breasts heaving as she tried to control her breath.

Klara grinned. "What?" she asked. "Never been topped before?"

And then Nic was wriggling her off, undoing her own jeans, and growling at Klara to take off her clothes before she ripped them off.

It was a battle to see who would be naked first and Klara lost. A loss that she was perfectly happy with as a fully naked Nic pushed her back onto the bed and stripped off her underwear with one hand.

"Wanna talk about being topped?" Nic asked.

Klara opened her mouth to respond, but Nic's hands were already parting her thighs, her mouth was already descending onto a hardened nipple, her fingers were already sliding up to meet the sticky wetness that had seeped out of her.

And all she could do was groan.

She'd been so close already, her heart pounding as Nic had been grinding against her. And to have all this sensation now, all at once, it was almost too much. Almost but not quite.

Nic sucked her and her fingers parted her lips and took the moisture there, circling up to her clit until Klara pushed her fingers into Nic's hair, pulling at it, pulling her down, forcing her to take more of her breast into her mouth. She groaned and her muscles clenched and there was no way she was going to be able to take more than thirty seconds of this. And just for once, she didn't care. She wasn't out to impress anyone. She closed her eyes and pushed her hips up so that Nic's fingers could slide into her and then she abandoned herself to it.

It came like a great crashing avalanche, pouring over her as she clenched and unclenched around Nic's fingers, as she cried out incoherently, as her breath left her completely and the world suddenly made complete sense to her. It was all for this moment. All for this. This is what life was supposed to be.

And then she was content, purring inside like a cat and could open her eyes and Nic was there, astride her, eyes still gleaming, lips swollen, full breasts tipped with hard nipples and Klara wanted her to have what she'd just experienced. Her hand slid down and Nic's was already there. She scooped underneath, letting her fingers linger for a second on wetness and then plunging inside as Nic stroked her clit.

In fast, eager, desperate movements Nic rode her hand, her breasts moving in rhythm as Klara watched and felt herself grow even wetter at the sight. She reached up, taking a nipple between her fingers and that was enough.

Nic moaned and then Klara felt a tightening around her fingers as Nic threw her head back and was engulfed by her climax. Klara held still, letting it happen, watching curiously as Nic became completely vulnerable.

And then it was over, Nic was lifting herself off Klara's fingers and they were sticky and breathless and sweating but far from done.

"I want to taste you," Nic said, coming close, whispering in her ear so that Klara shivered with delight.

"Lie down."

She moved herself so that they were side by side but top and tail, her face close enough to Nic that she could smell that strong musty odor again. And then Nic was pulling at her, parting her legs, forcing her face in between them, clutching at her ass as Klara felt the first warm, wetness of her tongue.

She moaned and then buried herself between Nic's legs, letting her tongue work rhythmically as Nic's did the same.

It was another contest that she lost. She was the first to be tipped over the edge, her face pushed up between Nic's legs, breathing in her scent as pulse after pulse of climax overcame her.

Chapter Eighteen

They were lying side by side on the bed, their legs tangled together. Nic studied the effect of her dark skin against the pale white of Klara's. Empty Chinese take out containers stood on the night stand. She could rarely remember feeling so... fulfilled. Content. Satisfied. She stroked Klara's hair back off her face.

"Still wanna quit?"

Klara sighed. "I probably should."

"You make that sound like a disaster."

Klara shuffled upward so that she was sitting up against the pillows. "Want the honest truth?"

"Yes."

"I need the money. My business needs the money. Not to mention the good press I'd get from doing a wedding for the Gainer family."

"Badly?" Nic asked.

"Badly enough," said Klara. "I mean, without it I might be able to squeak by with a loan or an investor or something."

"Your business means a lot to you." It wasn't a question. It was clear from the way that Klara spoke that her business meant everything to her, the way her face lit up when she talked about it.

"All I've ever wanted was a wedding," Klara said, smiling softly. "A wedding every day. Love every day. To be romanced, to be a part of romance. To make people happy. So yes, my business is important to me. And I'm getting there, I really am. More and more people are hearing about me and coming for appointments. Another six months, twelve max and I think I'll be standing on my own two feet and hiring an assistant. It's just a question of surviving until then."

Nic stroked a hand down Klara's pale thigh. "So don't quit then."

Okay, okay, getting her to quit or even firing her would probably make George happier with the idea that she was sleeping with the wedding planner. But she couldn't destroy Klara's business. Besides, she wasn't going to tell anyone else about all of this.

"That kind of depends," Klara said.

"On what?"

Klara sighed. "On this. What this is." She paused, looked down and Nic didn't say anything. She had a worried feeling in her stomach about what was about to happen. "You said maybe this was nothing, maybe it was just hormones," Klara said finally.

"Yeah." Again she didn't say more. She didn't know why, didn't know what exactly she was afraid of. That Klara would say it was just the sex, or that she'd say it wasn't.

Klara's eyes were bright blue when she looked up again. "There's something you should know about me."

Nic laughed, trying to take the seriousness away. "There's probably a lot I should know about you. We barely know each other. We've met, what, three times? I'm not saying that I never jump into bed with a woman on a first date, but I can definitely think of women I know better than you. What's your favorite ice cream flavor?"

Klara ran her tongue over her teeth and ignored the question. "I fall in love easily."

The words hung there. Nic began to digest them but wasn't done by the time she asked her question. "So this is... You want more?"

And again, she had no idea what she wanted out of this. It was only when Klara opened her mouth to start speaking that Nic realized that if she was being sent away, if this was all there was, she was going to be very disappointed indeed.

"I want more," Klara said. "But I'm not sure how or why or whether this can ever work at all."

"So, we date for a while," Nic said, secretly pleased now, wondering what had changed inside her to want this but not particularly caring.

"I told you, I warned you," Klara said. "I fall in love all too easily."

Nic sucked her bottom lip. What was Klara trying to say? She could figure that out if she wanted to, she just didn't want to think it. But in the end, did it matter? It wasn't like they were getting married or anything. Did it really matter what Klara thought or wanted or expected? What mattered was right now, the future could take care of itself. It always did in the end. So she pushed.

"What are you trying to say?"

Klara shook her head and smiled. "I'm trying to say that I'm already falling in love with you."

Nic's heart beat harder and she had to force herself to stay seated, not to spring up and start dragging her clothes on. The warmth of Klara next to her helped. The future could take care of itself, she reminded herself. What mattered was now.

SHE COULDN'T NOT SAY. She could see that Nic was hesitant and she knew that she could be overwhelming and too much, but she had to be honest. Nic had been honest with her and it was only fair. So despite the fear on Nic's face, despite the fact that she knew she should bite her tongue, she had to say what she said. Nic had a right to know. A right to know that if this continued then there was a chance it was going to get serious. Because that was the only kind of relationship that Klara could have. The only kind she ever had.

"You're falling in love with me?"

She blew out a breath. "I can't not tell you that. And if it helps, I fall in love with about three people a day."

For a long, long second, Nic stared at her. Then her face creased into a laugh. "Yeah, I guess that helps a little bit."

"I'm just saying, if you want to do this again, if this is something you want to pursue, if it's not just hormones, then it's something that you should keep in mind."

"The fact that you fall in love with anything that walks?"

Klara smirked a little. "Yeah, that pretty much sums it up."

"Alrighty then," Nic said, turning over so that they were facing one another. "Cards on the table time then, I guess. Is this a one time thing?"

"From my point of view, no," Klara said. "But that should have been pretty obvious. You?"

Nic studied her, then shook her head. "No. Definitely not just hormones. I thought maybe we could get it out of our systems, but to be honest, I just want you more than ever."

"Great, building a relationship on sex."

"Who said anything about a relationship?" Nic said.

"Well, I'm pretty sure that's what it's called when you don't just have a one-night stand but you keep seeing each other," Klara said. Then she laid a hand on Nic's arm, knowing she was getting anxious. "It's just a word, we can use another if you like. Like... affair maybe?"

"Affair. Huh. Okay," said Nic. "Well then, we're in agreement that we both want to continue seeing each other."

"Yes."

"Alright."

"Which means I probably should quit the wedding," Klara said, a sinking feeling inside as she said it.

"Which you can't afford to do," said Nic. She sighed. "I don't get why this is such a big deal. George is the same. I mean—"

"Wait, George knows about this?"

"He's one of my best friends, he guessed the second you walked into that first meeting that I liked you," said Nic. "And I get that that's weird, but yes, he knows. He's none too happy about it either."

"Understandable. If this wedding is going to go off without a hitch then you guys need to be the perfect couple."

She should leave this alone. The smart choice wasn't either/or, the wedding or the bride. The smart choice was neither. The smart choice was not getting involved with something so complicated. But that ship had sailed the second Nic's lips touched hers.

"Look, this is ridiculous. We're both adults," Nic said. "Why shouldn't we have everything? You do your job, arrange the wedding. I'll do mine, play the perfect bride when George's family is around. We'll get the wedding done, get the money and then we'll see what happens. In the meantime, you and I can, uh, get to know each other better."

"Like a secret relationship," Klara said. "Like an actual affair."

"Except the only person really being cheated on is George and he knows all about it," Nic said.

Klara looked down at her hands. It was tempting. Very tempting. She'd always tried to keep an open mind. If Nic was the one, then she had to be open to the idea of their relationship being a little... unorthodox. At least at the start. Right?

She could still feel Nic's hands on her skin, could feel those fingers inside her. She blew out a breath, then she nodded.

"We just have to be discreet. There's no reason this shouldn't work."

"What happens if we get caught?"

Nic rolled her eyes. "We won't get caught."

Nic's hands were already touching her again, pulling her in and they stopped her asking the question that was really on her mind. *What happens if I fall completely in love with you?* Nic's lips were on her shoulder and Klara groaned. This was fine, she told herself. Completely fine. She'd got what she wanted, a beautiful woman that was interested. So what if there were complications along the way. Every relationship had complications, right?

Nic's fingers were skimming over her hip bone and Klara wrapped her arms around her, pulling her in closer.

I might love you, she thought. But she didn't say it out loud.

Chapter Nineteen

She had never fallen in love.

Lust a few times, sure. In fact, more than a few times if she was being totally honest. But love? Never. The very idea of it made her feel shaky inside, like she'd eaten too many sno-cones. If she thought about what Klara had actually said, rather than the way she'd looked or the way she'd felt or the way she'd smelled, then she got dizzy and her stomach swirled. Which just meant it was more comfortable not to think about what Klara had said. Problem solved.

It wasn't like it was a pressing issue. She went to work, Klara planned the wedding, they talked on the phone, and twice in the last week they'd fallen into bed together. It was no different than most relationships Nic had been in. Though the word relationship might be stretching things a little. And okay, Klara could be... a little much.

She wanted detailed play-by-plays of the day, a day that had been the same as any other because all days were the same. She made sandwiches, dressed salads, got paid and that was that. And Klara always seemed to want to know what her plans were, always wanted to know where she'd be and when. But then again, perhaps she was just being careful, making sure they didn't run into anyone she knew, keeping their little affair under wraps.

Nic held the idea of Klara close to herself, like a precious gift. Yes, Klara could be overwhelming at times, but it wasn't like Nic had that much experience. Maybe that was how things were supposed to be. Besides, lying in Klara's arms, seeing her smile, holding her body, those things more than made up for it.

What about when they didn't? Nic didn't listen to the voice in the back of her head often, didn't see a point. The future was blurry and out of focus and she had enough to worry about right now without needing to practice her fortune-telling skills.

She stomped up the stairs to the apartment, back aching after standing in the kitchen all day and stinking of grease and the floor cleaner that she'd spilled over her sneakers. All she wanted was a shower and maybe a dirty phone call with Klara, something to get her through the night until their date tomorrow. Hell, she'd settle for a regular phone call. Klara's voice managed to calm her, and she definitely needed some calming.

She couldn't wait to quit this job. Couldn't wait to get a new start, really start to build something with her life. Something with potential, something she loved and that brought the money in too. Her heart beat a little harder at the thought of it. Maybe she'd actually feel like a grown-up at last. Pull this wedding off and she'd be free and clear and on her way to Europe on the next flight.

She opened the front door and nearly fell over a pair of black boots that she recognized as Sally's. Uh-oh. Sally was here with George, that couldn't be a good thing. There was silence in the apartment and she opened the living room door with some trepidation. They couldn't have killed each other, could they? Not on a Wednesday.

The door pushed open the rest of the way to reveal George, slouched in the armchair, face buried in his phone, and Sally at the end of the couch, flicking through a magazine as far as it was physically possible to get from George. It took a second before they looked up and saw her.

She blew out a breath. "What's all this then?"

"Come and sit down," said Sally.

George just nodded.

Nic slowly walked to the couch. Whatever was happening here it was weird and she wasn't sure she liked it. George and Sally would normally be at each others' throats right now.

"Is this some kind of intervention?" she said as she sat down.

"No!" George said. Then he shrugged. "Maybe. Kind of."

"And you're in on this?" she said, looking at Sally.

Sally put the magazine down. "I'm here to take you out for a drink," she said. "But as it happens, George has convinced me that you need a good talking to."

"George has?"

"Hey, I can be very convincing!"

Nic looked from one to the other and then shook her head. She had a feeling she knew what was coming and it made her angry. She calmed herself with the thought that they both cared about her. They were trying to do the right thing, trying to look after her. Even though she really didn't need looking after.

"It's about Klara," George started.

"Fine," said Nic. "Are we going to be talking about Tobias after then?"

"Hey, we're here because we care," Sally said.

And Nic caught just the hint of humor in her voice. So Sally wasn't completely on board with this idea then.

"And I see that look," Sally said. "As it happens, I do think that George has a point. This thing with Klara is dangerous and stupid."

"My two favorite adjectives," Nic said.

"Flirting with her, fine," said George. "Sleeping with her even. I can't say I was thrilled about it, but I guess you're an adult. But Nic, this is getting serious. You're either with her or talking about her or talking to her."

"Not true," Nic said, knowing immediately that it was true.

"It sounds to me like you're falling for this woman," said Sally. "Which is awesome, of course." She glared over at George who took the hint.

"Very awesome, very happy for you," he said, though Nic suspected his teeth were gritted.

"But we're worried that, um, that maybe you're letting your feelings blind you to other... realities." Those sounded like George's words coming out of Sally's mouth.

"You're worried," Nic said, trying to remind herself that they truly were, that they weren't just interfering.

George turned now, facing her straight on. "Nic, we are worried. I'm worried. Worried that we're going to screw up this whole plan."

"A plan that is still insane, by the way," added Sally.

George sighed. "I get it, you like her. A lot. Which is really good, honestly, I'm really happy for you, Nic. But... But I'm scared too. Scared that we're going to get caught, get found out. These people are my family."

"So what do you want me to do about it?" Nic asked. "Leave her? Call it quits? Because I think you know that isn't fair. I think you wouldn't leave Tobias if I just asked you to, if I just told you I was worried about you."

"No," George said, darting a glance over at Sally. "No, you're right. But the wedding is a couple of weeks away. Couldn't you... Couldn't you calm things down until then? I mean, after the wedding do whatever you like. But just until the actual thing takes place could you..." He trailed off.

Nic looked at Sally who shrugged. Then she sighed. George was a worry-wart. Always had been. And he was getting stressed. She could see the flare of a patch of eczema under his jaw line, always a sign that things were getting too much. The wedding, the thought of the money, lying to his family. And now here she was adding to his troubles by dating the wedding planner.

Even if she didn't intend to get caught doing so.

She took a breath before she nodded. "Fine."

George's face lit up and he jumped out of his chair to hug her and she couldn't help but laugh. It was nice seeing George happy, nice solving someone's problems with just one word. And it wasn't like she had to stop seeing Klara. She just had to be a little more discreet for the next couple of weeks. No big deal.

"Great," said Sally. "Time for a drink then. Let's get out of here."

Nic almost, almost protested, almost said that she was about to call Klara. But she stopped herself. A drink couldn't hurt. She could call Klara later, in private. "Fine, let me just get changed."

George was already grabbing his jacket, off to see Tobias, she was sure. But he hesitated before putting it on.

"Um, one thing," he said.

"Mmm?"

"I talked to mom today. She, uh, she's a little upset that she's not more involved with the planning and, well, I told her..." Again he trailed off. He looked at Nic pleadingly.

"You told her that she could help," Nic filled in.

George nodded and bit his lip.

"Isn't this the woman that hates you for being Latina?" Sally asked.

Nic nodded just as George said: "She absolutely doesn't. I don't know where you've gotten this idea from, she really, truly doesn't care. I swear she doesn't."

And he was starting to get upset again and Nic couldn't take it so she nodded reluctantly. "I'll give her a call. Okay?"

George beamed and danced out of the apartment.

"You placate him far too much," Sally said.

"What can I say? He's cute and I like his smile. Besides, he's there for me when I need it."

Sally grunted. "And now you have an interfering almost mother-in-law to deal with."

Which wasn't precisely the problem, Nic thought as they too left the apartment. The real problem was going to be dealing with George's mother and Klara in the same room. Jesus. What had she let herself in for?

Chapter Twenty

Klara stood back, blending into the background. Ideally, no one should notice her at a wedding. The dancing and persuading and flexing she did behind the scenes should be exactly that, behind the scenes. And just for once, absolutely everything was going to plan.

The bride shifted a little to get closer to her new husband and Jet click-click-clicked and the wedding party laughed and the sun shone and this, this was why she did this job. She smiled to herself and watched as the groom looped his arm around his wife and his parents kissed her cheeks and welcomed her to the family.

No dramas here. She went off into the restaurant to ensure that the food was laid out properly and everything was in order.

"I'm not convinced." Jet strode in ten minutes later, camera dangling from its strap.

Klara looked around. "Where are they?" She had sudden visions of a tornado scooping up the wedding party, or a tsunami roaring in.

"Calm your pants, they're doing some family pics, that's all. Everyone's getting the cell phone pictures out of the way so that they can come and eat."

Klara surveyed the room and nodded. Just right. "So, what aren't you convinced about?"

"You, having an affair. Out of everyone I know, you're the least likely to have an affair."

"Because?"

"Well, firstly because you fall in love too easily, and frankly, love can be a liability in an affair. And secondly because, well, because you're just too nice."

"You do know that it's not really an affair, right?" Klara said, straightening some napkins. "I mean, yes, she's getting married, but it's a sham marriage."

"I know that you're getting yourself involved in something that sounds an awful lot like complications you don't need."

Klara sighed. "Yes, in the cold light of day I get that this isn't exactly ideal. But I like her, Jet. Like, really like her."

"Why?"

It was such a simple question and it left her stumped. Not because she didn't have an answer, but because she couldn't put it into words.

"What makes this Nic so different from every other woman you've fallen in love with?" pushed Jet.

"She..." Klara sighed. "She makes me feel complete. I know that sounds ridiculous and I know I fall in love with just about everyone but I also know that this one feels different. More comfortable somehow. Like..."

"Like you were wrong every other time and this one is actually love?"

Klara shook her head. "No, not really. More like... Like every other time was practice, like every other time was just leading up to this. We've known each other for a few weeks, that's all, and I know I should take things slowly, I know this is complicated and not ideal and it's risky and all the rest of it. But I also know that I can't not do this. The feeling I get when she touches me..."

Jet perched on the edge of a table and Klara swatted at her arm until she stood up again. Klara straightened up the table cloth.

"You've got it bad, huh?"

Klara nodded.

Jet sighed. "Fine, I'm convinced. But this Nic had better be a goddess. I mean, seriously, she'd better be more than worth it."

"She is," Klara said, though she couldn't have said exactly why.

Jet reached for her hand and pressed it. "Affairs don't usually end well."

"This one will. This is different. This is not really an affair."

"Okay, okay."

There was the sound of the wedding party approaching the restaurant, laughs and chattering and happiness. Klara glanced over everything one more time. Perfect.

"What are you doing after this?" she asked Jet, who shrugged in response. "Swing back by the office with me."

"Why exactly?"

"Because Nic's coming to pick me up." Klara took a deep breath. "I think it's time that you two met."

Jet grinned. "You sure she's ready for that?"

Klara had a brief image of shaven-headed Jet arching her eyebrows at Nic in her leather jacket. Honestly, the meeting could go either way. "You gotta promise not to hit on her."

Jet rolled her eyes. "I seriously doubt that we have the same type. Besides, I'm into the D these days. My last three dates have been with guys, it's starting to become a habit."

"Well don't break that habit with Nic," Klara said. But she was joking, she knew Jet wouldn't do anything wrong, anything to jeopardize their friendship.

"It would be my honor to meet your beloved," Jet said.

At that moment the bride and groom entered the restaurant to a round of applause.

IT WAS strange to feel so nervous. But Jet was such an important part of her life, and she was hoping that Nic would be an important part of her life and therefore it had to be important that they could at least tolerate each other.

"Don't stress so much," Jet said, fiddling with camera lenses and putting them back into their slots in her bag.

"But what if you don't like her?"

"I will."

"What if she doesn't like you?"

"She will."

"You sound awfully confident."

"There's no other way to be," Jet grinned, zippering her bag shut and leaving it sitting in the corner of Klara's desk.

Klara sat down, then stood up again, her nerves too jangling to stay in one place.

"And it's not like you're marrying the girl," Jet said. "I mean, technically you're helping her get married, but that's different. And for once you haven't declared your undying love so there's that..." She trailed off as she saw the look on Klara's face. "Klara!"

"I didn't! I just said that maybe I was falling in love with her. I didn't actually say I loved her. I just—"

"Klara, you really need to wear less of your heart on your sleeve. You can't—"

Jet slammed her mouth shut as the door opened and Nic walked in. Klara felt a wave of comfort pass over her as she saw Nic, saw the curve of her smile, her familiar jacket. Suddenly, everything seemed like it was going to be okay again. No matter what Jet said. Her heart was beating hard, but she was in control of the situation.

"Hey," she said, standing up on tip-toes to kiss Nic's cheek. She felt a hand on her waist and her legs trembled. "Um, this is Jet, my best friend."

Jet was smiling and Nic's hand was reaching out and they were shaking hands and Klara could see from Jet's smile that things were going okay. She slipped away from Nic's arm.

"I'm just going to collect my things," she said. "I'll leave you two to get to know each other. Play nicely!"

And she escaped to the bathroom. She waited a good two minutes, checking her makeup and washing her hands and finally, grabbing her jacket from the hallway on her way back. As she opened the door she saw Jet and Nic so close that they were almost touching. Jet was speaking in a low voice, Nic was nodding solemnly.

"What's going on here then?" she asked.

"Not a thing," Jet said, stepping back.

"Nothing," said Nic at the same time. She held out her hand. "Shall we get out of here?" She didn't wait for an answer. "It was lovely meeting you, Jet."

"Likewise."

Jet dropped Klara a wink as they were turning to the door, and Klara stuck out her tongue.

"I'll lock up here," Jet said. "Don't you worry."

And then they were outside, Nic taking her hand and all was right with the world and Klara felt herself relaxing into things. Everything was natural. That was the difference. Okay, so maybe she shouldn't have told Nic that she was falling in love with her. But she had, and it had taken the weight off her, it had felt right. Most everything felt right with Nic.

"So, where are we going then?" she asked.

"Picking up take-out and heading to my place?"

Her heart jumped a little. "Okay," she said, a little too slowly.

Nic stopped and turned. "Uh, we could go out if you want?" she said, eyes concerned. "It's just, well, we don't want too many people seeing us right now, you know?"

A deep breath and a nod. "Sure, yes, of course. And, um, George?"

"Not home," Nic assured her.

Most everything felt right with Nic. But not everything. Still, relationships had to have compromises. In her pocket, her phone buzzed. She pulled it out to find a message from Jet.

Hot. Smart too. She's a winner. Have fun tonight xxx

She grinned and held Nic's hand a little tighter. Having Jet on-side made all the difference.

Chapter Twenty One

They were sitting side by side, backs propped up by the couch, the coffee table littered with take-out trays. It was comfortable. More comfortable than Nic could remember being. In general, she was looking for an angle, looking for her opening to get the object of her affections into bed. But not here, not with Klara.

Not that she didn't want to get her into bed. It was just that there felt like there was time. So much more time than normal. It was an odd feeling.

"You know, considering the fact that you're a cook I'm a little surprised that you haven't made me dinner yet," Klara said.

Nic grimaced. "I know, people always say that. Maybe one day, when I've got a great kitchen and all the things I need, maybe I'll have big dinner parties then."

"You don't exactly seem like a big dinner party person," Klara said.

Nic snorted. A dinner party. Not really her scene.

"Are you an only child?" Klara scooped up some chicken Korma.

"No."

There was a pause as Klara chewed. "Okay, um, does that mean that I shouldn't ask any more questions or that you're just lousy at being interviewed?"

Nic blew out a breath. Okay, she needed to open up a little. Fine. She could do that. Not the whole story, but some. "I'm the youngest of six," she said. "Typical tex-mex family. Catholic, lots of kids, way too much shouting at home."

"Uh-huh." Klara eyed her carefully. "I'm guessing you don't see them much?"

"I, um..."

"I'm planning your wedding," Klara said. "And there's a distinct lack of relatives on your side. So I assume..."

"That I got disowned when I came out?" Nic said, surprised that the words still hurt so much after so much time.

Klara nodded and Nic didn't want to pursue the conversation so she said: "What about you?"

"Only child, parents are gone. All alone in the big, bad city," Klara said.

"Except for Jet."

"Except for Jet," Klara agreed. She hesitated for a second, then asked: "While we're playing twenty questions, if you don't mind me asking, what was Jet talking to you about back at the office, you know, when I came back in?"

Nic laughed and picked up her fork again. "She was threatening me with violence. Said she'd stomp my head in if I so much as looked at you wrong."

"Oh God, I'm so sorry. I'll talk to her, she really wouldn't do that, you know? I swear. She likes you, she texted me and told me so, it was just—"

"Her way of being protective," Nic said. "It's fine. I get it."

And it was strangely fine. If anyone else had stepped up in her space like that she'd have shown them that she wasn't a girl to be messed with. But this had been different. Jet had seemed truly concerned. Concerned enough that Nic had felt a flutter of guilt in her stomach when she'd nodded and told Jet that there was nothing to worry about.

Guilt because whilst she didn't intend to hurt Klara at all she had no idea what was going to happen in the future. Guilt because Jet was already acting like the two of them were a couple. Which they kind of were, she guessed, but also kind of weren't. They weren't official. Things might end. Things could very well end.

And then she might be getting her head stomped in by Jet, which didn't sound fun.

"What about after the wedding?"

The question came out of the blue and the way Klara said it told Nic that she'd been thinking about it for a while, that she wanted to know but didn't want to seem nosy.

"George will move to LA, we'll hang out on holidays for a couple of years to show his parents, then we'll quietly get divorced."

"Okay." Klara frowned into her rice. "And you?"

Nic grinned. The idea still warmed her heart. A heart that for quite a while she'd thought was un-meltable. "Paris."

"Paris?"

"Paris. I'm going to up my game, learn how to cook better, get myself some qualifications. If I work hard enough, get a good reputation, then one day I might even own my own restaurant."

"In Paris?"

There was something about the way Klara kept saying the name, something that was off but Nic didn't quite know why.

"No, probably right back here in the city."

"Good."

It sounded sincere and relieved and suddenly Nic caught on. "You were worried I was going to emigrate?"

Klara shifted uncomfortably. "Um..."

Nic laughed. "Are we back to you falling in love too easily again?" she asked. "Because I'm not scared that you don't want me to leave. I'm not put off by the fact that you'd prefer me to live somewhere that's not an eight hour flight away."

"Really?"

Nic shrugged. It was kind of flattering actually. "Really." Then she remembered something. "There is something that I am scared of though," she said. "Something I need to tell you."

Klara put her plate down, sat up straighter, prepared herself for what was to come. "Go ahead. You can tell me anything."

"It's bad," warned Nic, feeling her mouth twitch into a smile.

"Oh, God. I'm ready. Tell me."

She leaned in close enough that her lips were tickling Klara's ear. "George's mother wants to come and taste menus with us tomorrow."

Klara leaned her head back and laughed, a sound that made Nic's heart beat harder. "You fool, I was getting really worried there for a second."

"Well, you should be worried. You haven't met George's mother yet."

"I deal with mothers-in-law all the time," Klara said. "I'll deal with her just fine."

And Nic was getting distracted now. Distracted by the smell of Klara's hair, by the softness of her skin, by the fact that she was so tantalizingly close. She moved a little closer, letting her lips dance over Klara's neck and felt a deep intake of breath.

Slowly, almost casually, she moved her hand, letting it linger on Klara's thigh for a second and then move upwards, feeling heat, feeling a trembling in her stomach as she sensed Klara responding to her.

She was just about to make her move, to push the coffee table aside, when Klara deftly caught both her wrists.

"Hey!"

"Hey yourself," growled Klara, turning around, keeping hold of Nic's wrists as she straddled her, pushing her back against the couch.

"I started this," Nic said.

"And you're moving entirely too slowly, so I'm taking over."

Her eyes were heavy-lidded and her mouth was swollen and Nic didn't usually like surrendering control but this, this was... She felt the wetness already starting to pool inside her, felt her breath coming faster. Klara leaned over, a blonde waterfall of hair covering Nic's face as she kissed her, sweetly, softly, slowly. And then deeply, passionately, wantingly.

"Want to take this to the bedroom?" Nic asked, pulling back a little.

"Hell no," said Klara. "I'm not sure I'd make it past the hallway."

Then Nic was pulling off her t-shirt and letting Klara handle her own, bras flew over the couch, and skin was touching skin and Nic pulled her in close, felt Klara's body pressed up against her own and Klara's hands were tangled in her hair, pulling at it and Nic was pulsing with need.

She buried her head in Klara's breasts, sucking and kissing and teasing as Klara's hips pushed into her and she could smell Klara's scent. She could smell her and feel her and taste her and she realized that in the space of a minute she'd gone from zero to sixty. She was close to coming already and Klara had barely touched her.

She laughed and Klara tilted her head back and that arched her back and pushed her breasts towards Nic's mouth and then she was far, far too busy to laugh.

IT WAS dark outside, the streetlights playing through the windows as they lay in a heap of clothes on the couch. Thank God George was spending more and more time at Tobias's. She'd have to make sure she picked up all the clothing. Nothing like a stray pair of underwear to give the game away. She felt a stab of guilt at betraying George's trust like this, but then, where was he? Safe in the arms of the man he loved. So... She held Klara close, drinking in her warmth.

"So, George's mother, huh?" Klara said sleepily. "Is she a real dragon?"

"She hates me," Nic confirmed. She lazily stroked Klara's arm. "This is going to be okay, right?"

"What?"

"This, me and you and meeting George's mom tomorrow?" There was a quick pang of worry now. "I mean, we're going to have to be careful, discreet, no touching, no... no funny business."

There was quiet in the darkness for long enough that Nic thought maybe she'd fallen asleep.

"It'll be fine," Klara said finally.

"It has to be fine," said Nic. "Really, truly fine. We can't screw this up."

Danger seemed closer now that her hormonal needs had been sated. She could see a little more clearly what George had been so worried about. It was all very well saying that she could control herself, probably she could. But could Klara? Could Klara keep her hands to herself, could she prevent herself giving secret little smiles?

"It'll be fine," Klara said again.

Nic snuggled against her, breathing in the smell of her hair. It would be fine. It had to be.

Chapter Twenty Two

The caterer was one of the most popular in the city and Klara had had a standing contract with them for as long as she'd been in business. The process was streamlined. They provided tasting menus, the clients tasted and decided, she placed the order. Of course, there was the odd wedding that needed something out of the ordinary, in which case she might call someone else in, but in general, this was the caterer of choice. The point being, they had a quality product. She knew they did. If they didn't, she wouldn't have been using them for the last few years.

She was just straightening some knives and forks when the door opened and Nic entered. Her instinct was to swoop into her arms, kiss her, feel her. But she held herself back, smiling politely from the other side of the table.

"Good afternoon," she said carefully.

"It's fine, you've got about two minutes while she's busy bitching out the town car driver for running a yellow light."

"It can't be that bad."

"Oh, it is," Nic said. "She is. Trust me on that."

There was nothing that Klara wanted more than to comfort her. The memory of last night burned into her brain and for perhaps the first time she saw how uncomfortable their situation could be. She wanted to kiss Nic, to touch her, to remind herself of her scent. But she couldn't.

"I'm sure everything will be just fine," she said. "I told you. Tons of experience in the general mother-in-law area. We'll be all good."

Nic grimaced. "You've been warned."

Klara was grinning at her when the door opened and she had to hurriedly re-arrange her face into a more lady-like smile. This time she did move, skirting the table and holding her hand out.

"Mrs. Gainer, I've heard so much about you."

The woman was tall, thin and almost angular. She had the kind of bone structure that spoke of younger beauty. Hell, she was attractive now, her eyes carefully made up, her grey-white hair carefully styled. Her nose was thin and she sniffed as she took Klara's hand.

"Not quite the area of town I was expecting," she said.

Nic raised an eyebrow at Klara as if to say 'I told you so.'

Klara decided to ignore the insult. She smiled more widely. "I hope you had a pleasant drive over."

Mrs. Gainer tutted. "Drivers nowadays. Really, the rules of traffic are perfectly simple, I don't see why it's so difficult to stop at a changing traffic light."

Klara took a deep breath. Okay, okay, George's mother was a pill. She got it. She was just going to have to keep her patience and keep smiling. Nic was still pulling faces and she couldn't help but think that this whole thing would be a hell of a lot easier if Nic weren't there. But then, her life would be a hell of a lot easier if Nic weren't actually getting married at all.

"If you'd like to take a seat," she said, standing back to give them access to the table. "We generally start with a presentation of the hors d'oeuvres and make our way through to dessert. I've ensured that there is a notepad and a pen so you can jot down any thoughts that you have."

George's mother picked up the pen, a regular old ballpoint, and sniffed again. "I'll use my own," she said, opening up her handbag and sliding out a silver pen.

"Jesus Christ," Nic said.

Klara took another deep breath, pulled out Mrs. Gainer's seat, and scowled at Nic. This was going to be even more difficult if Nic wasn't able to keep her temper.

"We're looking for a selection of three hors d'oeuvres," Klara continued in an attempt to keep the peace. "As well as two starter courses, two main courses, and a dessert. So if we could keep that in mind, it would be helpful."

Mrs. Gainer's nose wrinkled. "Where on earth did you find this woman?" she said to Nic, not even trying to keep her voice down.

"She was on the list that you suggested," Nic began.

"I can't think why."

Klara's stomach clenched. As if she didn't already feel bad enough with her business almost failing. The one bright spot had been that the Gainers had chosen her for their wedding. Apparently, that hadn't been a planned decision though. She felt her hands start to shake and her cheeks begin to color. She kept silent, expecting Nic to say more, but she didn't. She was rescued only when one of the catering staff came in, holding a large tray with a selection of mouth-sized snacks.

"Wow," Nic said. "These look delicious."

It took two and a half minutes for Mrs. Gainer to turn her nose up at every possibility. "Not at all what we had in mind."

Klara turned to Nic, but she was looking at George's mother.

"My husband and I are paying for this wedding," Mrs. Gainer added.

Klara swallowed. "I'll talk to the caterers and ask them to add more options," she said. "If you'd like to re-arrange a date to come and taste them?"

Mrs. Gainer harrumphed, a noise that Klara had never heard before. "I simply don't have the time. I'll ask my own caterers to arrange the hors d'oeuvres."

Klara wondered how the hell she was going to square that with her own company, but she said nothing, let the staff clear away the tray and bring in tasters for the actual menu.

"No, no, no," Mrs. Gainer said, after only a look. She turned to Nic. "You really should have gone with one of the bigger planners. Someone with good contacts."

Klara could already feel tears pricking at her eyes. She blinked them away. Nic was thin-lipped and stiff, but she said nothing.

"I'm fairly sure this dessert came out of a package," Mrs. Gainer continued, stirring what Klara knew was a chocolate mousse made by hand. "And honestly, chicken or salmon? Could the choices be any more banal?"

"Mrs. Gainer," Nic began.

But it was too late now. She was on a role.

"I'm sure you're a lovely person," Mrs. Gainer said, turning ice-blue eyes onto Klara. "But it's clear that you simply have no idea what you're doing here. This wedding is out of your league, it's that simple."

The tears were burning again. She swallowed but her throat felt full and tight. Why the hell was she letting this woman get to her like this? And there was Nic, still silent, not defending her or saying a thing.

"If you want to keep our business, I'm afraid you're going to have to do an awful lot better than this."

And she saw an escape route. She had to get out of here before the tears escaped, before she embarrassed herself.

She gave a sick smile. "Let me just go and check with the caterers. Perhaps they have another menu that would be more to your taste."

She fled, making it out of the door and into the corridor before the first tear rolled down her cheek. She choked back a sob, trying to control herself. She hadn't known that George's parents were paying for all this. She'd assumed that Nic was, that she'd chosen her. And now she was apparently not up to the job.

The door opened and Nic slid out, closing the door quickly.

"What's going on?" she hissed.

And Klara snapped.

"You could have said something, could have defending me in there, instead of letting that arrogant, horrible woman stomp all over me."

"Jesus." Nic came closer. "Klara, I'm sorry. I told you she was terrible."

"I don't know what was worse," Klara said through her tears, not thinking straight. "The fact that she doesn't think I can plan a wedding, or the fact that you couldn't find a word to say in my defense."

"Klara, I was being careful, I was being discreet." She came closer still, pressing up against her. "And mostly, I was trying to hold on to my temper. I knew that if I said one word then all the rest would come spilling out."

"And then she'd know our secret."

Nic nodded. "I'm sorry. I didn't know she'd upset you so much."

Klara sniffed and blinked. She was being stupid. She was a professional with a job to do and she needed to get it together. And Nic was standing so close. Almost automatically she turned her face to Nic's.

Their lips met and Klara calmed and she could do this. Nic's arms came up and enveloped her and she really could do this. Keeping things secret sucked, George's mother sucked, but this, this was what was important.

Neither of them heard the door open.

But both of them heard Mrs. Gainer's shrill voice. People in Philadelphia heard Mrs. Gainer's shrill voice. Quite possibly, people in LA heard Mrs. Gainer's shrill voice.

"You're fired!"

The door slammed closed again and Nic's arms dropped away and suddenly Klara felt very, very cold.

Chapter Twenty Three

One god-damned kiss. One. They'd been so careful, so discreet and now... She reined in her anger, took a deep, shuddering breath. Why the hell had she followed Klara out into the hall? Why the hell had Klara walked out on a business meeting anyway? Okay, maybe she was upset, but she was a professional, surely.

She was shaking now, time passing far too slowly, just standing in the corridor and not even looking at Klara. What had she done? Everything was ruined now. Everything. And Klara was mad because she didn't jump to her defense in front of George's mother. How very... Klara. George's mother. George. Oh, shit.

"We need to..." she started.

But then she did look at Klara and she saw the white, frozen shock on her face, saw the tears that weren't yet leaking down her cheeks and saw fear.

"What?" The word came out sounding sharp. But she hadn't quite decided that she wasn't angry with Klara yet. It was Klara's fault they were out here, Klara and her ridiculous ideas about what a relationship should be, that Nic should be her knight in shining armor, willing to risk it all to defend a maiden who, truth be told, could have defended herself.

"Nic, I—" Klara's voice choked.

She was obviously upset. But hell, so was Nic. This whole plan had depended on her being discreet on keeping secrets and... and thinking ahead and being careful and doing things that she wasn't necessarily good at. As George might have tried to point out. George. She needed...

"Nic, I'm so sorry, I can't even... I don't know..."

Big blue eyes looked up at her and Nic could feel herself melting a little, could feel the anger abating, her normal self coming back. She was still shaking, heart still pounding. But it was fear more than anything. She took a deep breath.

"It's done," she said.

"But... but what about the wedding and the money and George and... and my business," Klara finished in barely a whisper.

Nic's head was whirling now, she was thinking, like a rat caught in a maze she was trying to come up with any possible method of escape.

"She can't have seen much," she said, barely aloud. "I mean, my back was to her. She couldn't have seen exactly what was happening."

"Then why fire me?" Klara said. "And why storm out of here?"

Nic took another deep breath. "I don't know. But... But I think we have to find George."

Hurriedly, she pulled her phone out and keyed in his name. The phone rang and rang, but there was no answer. "Come on," she said, shoving the phone in her pocket.

Klara was leaning against the wall.

"Come on," Nic said again.

"Without this, I'm going bankrupt," Klara said, her lips hardly moving, her face still pale and white.

"Then let's damn well fix this," Nic said. She reached out and pulled at Klara's arm, but Klara didn't move. "Jesus, you were so eager for me to defend you before and now I'm telling you that we need to act, that we need to fix things and you won't even..."

"It's too late," said Klara. "Maybe we should just let things go. Maybe—"

"Maybe you're willing to admit defeat, but I'm not. If you don't want to come, then fine." She turned to walk away.

She was half-way down the stairs when Klara caught her up. "I'm sorry."

"Nothing to be sorry for," Nic said. "We're both in this up to our necks. The only thing we can do is try to fix what we did. And George is our first stop."

Klara said nothing, but Nic felt a sense of comfort having someone there, being followed, knowing that whatever happened at least Klara was with her. Okay, they might be spending the night on the street, or at least be on the verge of losing everything, but they had each other. Her anger was gone now. Replaced by gnawing fear and guilt. As they got into the cab, she took Klara's hand and squeezed it tight.

This was fixable. Probably. She just had to come up with a patch, that was all.

GEORGE SLAMMED the phone down when they walked in.

"I've been calling you."

"Sorry," Nic said. "I've been on silent. Listen—"

"No, I don't need to listen. I've been on the phone with my mother chewing my ear off for the last half an hour, what the hell were you thinking?"

"I—"

"Not you, for once," George said. He turned to Klara. "Given that Nic says you actually need this job, I'd have thought that you'd go a little further to keep it."

Klara's breath was coming faster and Nic could hear it and she had a sudden feeling of things falling into place, a sense that maybe things were going to work out. She felt stronger now. But Klara obviously didn't.

"George," she said carefully. "What exactly did your mother say happened this afternoon?"

"That she was shown to a half-rate restaurant, her words, not mine, and given inedible snacks, again, her words, not mine, and that the wedding planner walked out half-way through the tasting and..."

Nic blocked out the rest, relief making her deaf to George's words. She hadn't seen. She should have known better. There was no way George's mother could have seen the kiss from where she was standing. Nic had blocked her view. She blinked, aware suddenly that George was staring at her in silence.

"Well?" he said.

"Well what?"

"I asked you what the hell really happened? I can see by the look on your face that something did."

She took a heartbeat. She didn't have to tell him. But she did. He was her friend. He deserved to know the truth. She'd screwed up, and she wasn't going to compound the problem by lying about it. In brief words she sketched what had happened and George's face paled and he fell onto the couch.

"Jesus, Nic."

"It was half my fault," Klara began, her first words.

"No," George said. "It was Nic. I've known her a long time. Too long. This is pure Nic. Do what you want and the consequences be damned."

"That's not fair," she said, knowing damn well that it was.

"Really?" George asked. "Because you were thinking about our wedding, about our plan, about everything I have to lose, when you were kissing your wedding planner with my mother in the next room?"

"Maybe not," she allowed.

"But by pure luck, the kind of luck only you have, everything worked out in your favor again. Which means you won't learn your lesson again," George said.

She sat down beside him. "I will. I have. I was stupid, George. I—"

"I was just as stupid," Klara said, coming to sit on George's other side. "I deserve to be fired."

"What were you going to do?" George asked. "If you came here and my mother had seen you and..."

"We'd have jumped on a plane to Vegas and got married immediately," Nic said. It had been the best plan she'd come up with on the way there.

George snorted a laugh. "That the best you could do?"

"It could have worked," she said.

"And I expected better of you," George said, turning to Klara.

Klara blushed. "I've had my punishment already. I've lost the job that I needed. So maybe we can go a little easy on me for a while?" She looked over at Nic and her face softened. "And I'd like to say that it wasn't worth it, but it was."

"What was?" George asked, puzzled.

"Nic was. Is. She..." Klara turned to George and Nic saw how her face glowed and love shone from every pore and her stomach twisted and the hair on her arms stood up. "She's amazing," Klara said. "I wish I could do better than that, explain better than that. But she's comfortable and perfect and she makes me angry and happy at the same time and I don't want to have another morning without opening my eyes to see her there with me. Does that sound stupid?"

George shook his head, eyes shining. "No," he said softly. "No, it doesn't."

And Nic knew he was thinking about Tobias and knew now that he was really in love and knew too that Klara was. With her. And her heart grew a size and her skin tingled but inside there was a shadow of fear. Because how could she live up to someone like Klara's expectations?

"Listen, let me talk to my mother," George was saying. "Maybe I can persuade her that she'd be silly to fire you."

"How?" Nic asked, distracted from her thoughts.

"The wedding is almost planned, we'd have to pay most of what we owe to Klara anyway for the work she's already done, and you, my dear, as the blushing bride-zilla are insisting that Klara is the only planner you'll work with. That's an attitude that my mother will understand."

He picked up his phone from the table and walked out.

"I'm sorry," Klara said. "For all of this. If I hadn't left the room then we wouldn't be in this mess."

"No, I'm sorry. If I'd have been a little more pro-active and on your side, then you wouldn't have been so upset that you had to leave," said Nic. "And I am really, truly sorry."

Klara shuffled up, closing the gap between them. Nic's fears were fading into the background. She could handle Klara being in love with her. Hell, maybe she'd even fall in love with Klara. Stranger things had happened.

Klara took her hand and then Nic was leaning in, and then they were kissing again. It was a long time before they heard George clearing his throat in the door-way.

Chapter Twenty Four

She'd escaped by the skin of her teeth. She clicked through links, opening new tabs and letting her eyes flow over the search results.

It was all very well and good pretending that she was a grown up capable of running a business and carrying on a forbidden relationship, pretending that she could keep secrets and hide things. But the truth was, it grated on her.

Grated on her enough that when George had finally convinced his mother that she should re-hire Klara or lose her deposit, Klara had begged off drinks and a potential night with Nic to go home and brood.

Sun shone through the small office window. The office that she'd come so close to losing just yesterday. She'd woken up with a new sense of drive. Okay, she was probably being stupid, and the risks were obvious, but what was done was done.

What was extremely clear though was that if she really cared about the business she'd spent so long building up, so long wanting for herself, then she had to be more driven. Thus the search results on the screen in front of her.

Investment seemed way out of reach. As far as she could tell, people invested in products and companies way larger than her own. Okay, she could potentially show off her discount wedding bundles as a product, but still, serious investment just didn't seem like an option.

A loan could work. But she was still hesitant about asking for money that she might not be able to pay back.

Which didn't exactly leave a lot of options. She started clicking through the tabs that she'd opened, stuff that looked interesting, intriguing even. And then slowly began to close them one by one as they proved to be way less helpful than she'd thought.

The problem was that there was only one of her. She only had so much time and could only be in one place at once. Taking on extra work and getting more money was great, in theory. Right up until she realized that she'd double-booked an appointment and had to let someone down. There was a limit to what she could do alone. And it had become apparent that if she wanted the business to be on a more secure footing, then she needed to expand, get bigger and then the little things would matter less.

She closed another link, a page promising her huge investment for a small initial down-payment. Obviously a scam.

In the back of her mind she knew that she was avoiding thinking about Nic. All this work needed to be done, she wanted to save her business, but she also wanted not to think about Nic for a while. Because she got confused. Because just when she thought she'd decided enough was enough she thought of Nic's smile and changed her mind. Because just when she thought that she'd finally found a woman to love completely, she thought of Nic's wedding and changed her mind.

At least business was something she had some kind of control over. Theoretically.

She closed another tab and moved on to the next one.

She scanned the first few lines then drew herself up, skipping back to the beginning and reading again more carefully, leaning toward the screen and frowning. She was reading the article through for a third time when the door opened.

"Coffee service."

Jet bumped the door closed with her hip and placed two cups of coffee on the desk before ditching her camera gear, pulling out a chair, and putting her feet up on the desk.

"And a very good morning to you too," Klara said with a grin as Jet made herself comfortable.

"So, what's new, pussycat?"

For a second, Klara contemplated not telling her. But she couldn't. Jet was her friend, but more than that she was her sounding board, and not telling her would feel like some kind of betrayal.

"I nearly got us put out of business yesterday," she said as casually as she could.

Jet raised an eyebrow. "Um, you should probably elaborate on that."

Klara sighed and told her what had happened and Jet shook her head and picked up her coffee.

"You're playing with fire and I keep telling you that and I feel like you're not really listening."

"Yes, but—"

"But there's always a but," Jet said. "I know you like her, I know you think you love her, but just how much are you willing to risk? You came pretty close to not only destroying your business, but getting a terrible reputation as well. That's not smart, Klar."

"I know it wasn't smart. I know." She picked up her coffee. "But I also know that in a couple of weeks the wedding will be over and then—"

"Aha!" Jet said.

Klara practically spilled her coffee. "Aha what?"

"Aha, that's exactly what I'm building up to."

"Which is?"

"Which is, what happens after? Have you thought about that? Have the two of you talked about it?"

"What do you mean?" Stupid question, but she was playing for time, digesting the fact that now Jet brought it up, she and Nic hadn't done anything of the kind.

"I mean that I hear a lot about how great she is, I see that you adore her, and hell, I've met her myself and she seems pretty kick-ass. But as far as I know you're arranging her wedding to a man that wants to inherit some cash in order that they split the money. At which point, he's going to go do something somewhere, and she's going to go off to Paris and learn cooking or something."

"Right," Klara said, a cold shiver running down her back as she realized where this was going.

Jet put her coffee down and arched her eyebrow again. "You're not stupid, Klar. I know you know. I know you know what I'm telling you, and I know you know what I'm about to ask you. But you're trying not to think about it."

"No!"

"Fine then," said Jet with a sigh. "Where are you in all this then? What happens to you when Nic swans off to Paris? What plans do you have after this wedding? It seems like Nic and George know what they're doing."

Klara took a drink to stall. But Jet just stared at her and she obviously wanted an answer. And Klara couldn't be anything but truthful.

"I don't know."

Jet picked up her coffee again. "You can't just ignore the things that you don't like or that you don't want to think about," she said. "You do know that being in love with someone means dealing with everything? Sure, you like their smile, but you have to deal with them clipping their toenails in the bathwater too."

Klara had a mental image of Nic in the bath tub and a stab of lust went through her. "Yes, I know that."

"So, you and Nic need to have an uncomfortable conversation then. About what happens when all this wedding stuff is done. About the future. Or you need to pull back now, before it's too late, before you're in so deep that leaving her will hurt too much."

Jet's voice was kind and soft and Klara found herself nodding. Jet was right. "I'll take care of it. I swear."

"Tonight?"

She waited a second then nodded reluctantly. "Fine. Tonight." She drank more coffee. "Enough about me. What about your love life?"

Jet grunted. "Don't get me started."

"That bad, huh?"

"I'm so over guys right now."

"Go back to women then," Klara said, grinning.

"I might just do that," said Jet.

Something flashed on the computer screen, an email had come in, drawing Klara's attention for a second, reminding her of what she'd been doing before Jet arrived. She looked at the open website again, then turned the monitor toward Jet.

"What do you think of this?"

Jet peered at the screen. "What is it exactly?"

"It's a new funding platform. Sort of crowd-funding. It's divided up into cities and small local businesses can put themselves on the app and people can choose to donate or invest. It's a way of keeping cities vibrant, stopping the big corporations taking over."

"Huh. Smart plan." She looked up at Klara. "You thinking of listing yourself?"

"Maybe."

Jet nodded. "Do it. You might get a little financial help, which is always nice. But you'll also get your name out there, think of it as an advertisement for your services. It can't hurt to try."

"It's not like I'm expecting thousands of bucks here."

"No, but every little bit helps. Multiple strings to your bow and all that. Plus, you should get a nice reputation boost from the Gainer wedding, so there's that too."

The Gainer wedding. Put that way it sounded so impersonal, so unreal, so manageable. Nic's wedding. That sounded worse. So much worse.

"Yeah, right," she said. "Every little bit helps."

She was already starting the registration process when Jet rushed out to her next appointment.

Chapter Twenty Five

She stretched her legs out under the coffee table, scrolling through the options on her phone. "What about Italian?"

"Sure," said Klara.

It was the third word she'd said since Nic had walked in the door and she knew that something was wrong but she figured she'd try ignoring it first. If that didn't work, well, she'd come up with a plan B. For the time being she was being bright and cheerful and determinedly up-beat.

"Or Chinese?"

Silence. She glanced over out of the side of her eye and Klara was looking so pale that she softened. She took a deep breath and put her phone down.

"Listen, it was a close call," she said. "I get it. I was scared too. But it's dealt with now and the wedding is on and your business is safe and we just have to make it through the next couple of weeks, that's all."

Thank all the gods for George's skills of persuasion. And to be fair, his mother's forgiveness. The woman might hate her, but at least she'd done right by Klara.

"I know, I know," said Klara.

The clouds were still there, blocking the sun. Nic swallowed. She didn't want to do this, but it was clear that she had to. She had to at least offer. She sniffed. "Um, if you don't want to do this anymore," she began.

"No, no, it's not that." And Klara was looking panicky enough that Nic believed her.

"I don't mean for good," she said. "Just for right now. If you want to put things on hold for a couple of weeks, I'd totally get that. Totally understand."

"And after two weeks?" Klara said. "After the wedding?"

Nic stared at her, puzzled. "Uh, I guess we could go back to... to this. If you wanted to, I mean." She was confused. Klara was concerned about something, and that something had to do with the wedding, but what exactly she wasn't quite getting.

"I don't want to call things off," Klara said eventually in a small voice.

"Thank God," Nic said. She grinned and picked up her phone again and started looking for take-out. She was starving.

Klara could be... clingy, was the word she'd decided on. Wanting to know every detail of her day, wanting to be defended in front of George's mother. It took some getting used to. Particularly for someone as independent as Nic. But she could accept that this was an issue they both needed to work on. Klara needed to be less needy and Nic needed to be more considerate. How hard could that be? Every relationship needed compromises, surely?

"I don't want to call things off," Klara said again, more loudly this time. "I want to know what happens after."

Nic's pulse sped up. She thumbed through more restaurants on her phone, heart aching and fear making her mouth run dry. Only when it became apparent that Klara wasn't going to speak, wasn't going to stop staring at her, did she finally say anything.

"What do you mean?"

No need to over-react. Maybe Klara just meant the honeymoon. After all, it wasn't like she'd mentioned the word 'future' at all so far. Still though, Nic could feel her hands sweating.

"I mean after all this is over," Klara said. "I mean when George goes off to Los Angeles and you go off to Paris. What then? Where am I in this future that you've already decided on?"

And there it was. The F word.

"You know, we could do Thai," Nic said. "I'm kind of in the mood for noodles. What do you think?"

"I think that you're trying very hard not to take part in this conversation. I think that I'm hurting and confused and you're not helping me. I think that you know you and I need to talk about some things, but you're hoping that if you ignore me then I'll let things go and you'll be safe for another day."

"That's a no on the noodles then?"

Crap. So not the right thing to say. Klara got up, was walking away. Nic breathed slowly.

"Sorry," she said, as Klara reached the door. "Sorry."

Klara turned back. "Nic, you can't just avoid things you don't like. I'm a person, I have feelings and plans and all kinds of things. I'm asking you where I fit in with what you have planned for yourself. I'm asking if this, if me and you, is sustainable."

Nic put her phone on the coffee table. "I could get hit by a bus tomorrow," she said. "And then we've spent all evening arguing about a future that doesn't exist."

"And you might not get hit by a bus tomorrow," countered Klara.

"Why do we have to do this? Why can't you just take things as they come? No expectations, no plans. Whatever's going to happen will happen, no matter what plans we make, so why bother? Let's just enjoy what we have right now. Don't you enjoy what we have?"

Klara looked at her and her eyes were blue and her lips were kissable and those blonde bangs were brushing her eyelashes and Nic's heart just about skipped a beat. She had feelings, no matter whether she chose to admit them or not, she did have them. She just wasn't ready to name them yet, to risk getting hurt yet.

"I don't enjoy everything we have," Klara said. "I don't enjoy being your secret. I don't enjoy that we can never go out together in public. I don't enjoy feeling like you're ashamed of me."

"You know that isn't true," Nic said. "You know why we're keeping all of this secret."

"So that's going to change after the wedding?" Klara asked.

"Sure," said Nic, not entirely sure at all. She supposed she'd still have to be somewhat discreet, since George's parents and friends and contacts were all over the city.

"I'm not so sure," said Klara.

She sounded so sad that Nic took her hand, pulling her in closer, pulling her down so that she was sitting beside her on the floor. Then she had an idea.

"Then come out with me next weekend."

"What?"

Klara's face was so surprised that Nic smiled. "My friend Sally has been planning a hen party. Nothing huge. Just some drinks and dancing. Why don't you come too? I don't exactly know that many people, so it won't be crazy. Bring Jet if you'd like, if it'd make you more comfortable to know someone else there. She seemed pretty nice."

"Are you serious?"

"Serious," she said, squeezing Klara's hand. "Take it as proof that things will change. That I'm definitely not ashamed of you in any way, shape or form. And besides, I'd like you to be there." Only as she said it did she realize that it was true. "I'd really like you to be there."

"I don't know, it seems... weird."

"Any weirder than the rest of our relationship has been so far?"

Klara was smiling now, her eyes dancing. "I guess not."

"So it's a date then?"

Klara nodded. "I'll ask Jet too."

"The more the merrier," Nic said.

A weight lifted off her. The moment was gone, the F word had been mentioned but avoided. Even she could plan as far ahead as next weekend. Most importantly, Klara was smiling again.

"Now, about that food?"

"Noodles are great by me," Klara said.

Nic scrolled through her phone until she found the place she wanted and made their order. When she was done, she noticed that Klara too was glued to her phone. "What are you up to over there?"

"Just checking LocalVest," Klara said, eyes on the screen.

"Local what?"

Klara laughed and shifted over. "It's an app where people can support local businesses with donations or investments. I listed my company, figured I could use all the help I could get."

"Wow, are things that bad?"

"No, no," Klara said. "Just after the other day, well, I got a fright and... And I thought I should be more pro-active."

"Cool. I get it. And what else is new in your world?"

See, she could compromise. She could ask questions, could be interested, could even sometimes believe that this could work out. Sometimes.

The problem was that Klara had spotted the problem. The problem that should have been very obvious from the beginning and yet hadn't been. Hadn't been because Nic hadn't spared a thought to anything other than what she wanted in the moment. Just like George had warned her. Just like she always did.

Where did Klara fit into her Paris plans? Should they go together? Could Klara leave her business and waltz off to Paris? Did Nic even want her there? Paris was a chance to change everything. She didn't know if she could take her past with her and still have it work, still have a new life.

She did know, as she listened to Klara tell her about her day, that right now she was warm and happy and comfortable and didn't want to be anywhere else in the world.

But how could she say how she'd feel tomorrow? Or next week? Or next month?

Chapter Twenty Six

It had been a long time since she'd gone anywhere that required her to wear something not wedding-suitable. She had a closet full of suits and they hung there, taunting her. She couldn't wear a suit to a nightclub. Or wherever the hell they were going.

Her heart skipped a little as she thought of Nic, hair swinging, skin bathed in sweat, gyrating to music, her rhythm perfect.

No, definitely no suit.

She sighed and pulled out a pair of skinny jeans that she'd never worn. Now all she needed was to fit into them. She took a deep breath before she pulled them on.

She was looking forward to this. Really, she was. But. There was the but. She was looking forward to this but she was nervous as all hell. Maybe just because she was being taken out of her element. The jeans buttoned and she could even breathe. She grinned and reached for a top.

"Well, hello there." Jet cocked her hip against the doorframe and surveyed Klara's outfit.

"Where have you been?" Jet was supposed to be helping.

"Getting a little pre-game action going on," Jet said, swirling a glass. "Want some?"

Klara nodded and took the glass, feeling the burn of alcohol as she swallowed. Dutch courage. "Thanks," she choked, handing the glass back.

"You scrub up nicely," Jet said. "Going all out to impress Nic, huh?"

Klara looked in the mirror. Behind her, Jet was dressed as usual, all in black, boots, plenty of eye makeup. She looked like she'd fit in anywhere in the city. "Is this too much?"

Jet shook her head. "You look amazing. Throw on some heels and no one will be able to resist you."

As long as Nic couldn't resist her, that's what counted. She wanted Nic to want her, wanted her to be unable to keep her hands off her. Not that she doubted Nic's interest. It was just... Being in public. She understood why they had to be careful, but this was different. Nic had invited her out. There was no way that George's mother was hiding in a corner of a club waiting to catch them. Which meant that for once, Nic didn't have to be so cautious. Right?

She picked up an eyebrow pencil and Jet sprawled on the bed, carefully keeping her boots dangling over the edge. "So how did it go then?" she asked.

"How did what go?" She bit her tongue in concentration.

"The big conversation. You've been awfully slim on the details, kiddo. Did you or did you not discuss the future with Nic?"

Klara put the pencil down, picked up another. "Yes," she said. Then reconsidered. "No."

"Clear as mud." Jet sat up straighter. "Klar, you know why this is important, you know—"

"I tried!" She smudged her eyebrow with an index finger. "I tried, Jet. But... But she didn't want to and—"

"And you have no clearer idea of where you stand," finished Jet.

"It's not like that."

"Then how is it, exactly?"

Klara took a deep breath. How was it? That was a good question. She was no fool, she knew that Nic was avoiding talking about the future. She wished she could say why. Maybe the thought of the wedding was distracting her from everything else, which was fair. Maybe she had commitment issues. Strike that, she definitely seemed to have some kind of commitment issues.

Or maybe she just didn't like Klara as much as Klara liked her.

A lump of sadness rose in her throat.

"I don't know," she finally said.

"Let me ask you something then. What does your future look like? I mean, honestly. Realistically."

Klara carefully outlined her eyes in grey pencil before she answered. "Successful. Happy. I don't know."

"Try harder. Where do you see yourself five years from now?"

Klara sighed and turned to face Jet. "In charge of my own business, I guess. Going to weddings, planning weddings, maybe with an assistant or two."

"And how does Nic fit into all that? Does she fit into all that?"

"Of course," Klara said immediately. "I won't work all the time. She'll have her job, we'll live together, maybe get a dog."

"Stop right there."

"Why?"

"Do you see how easy that was?"

Klara shrugged. "I guess."

"You can slide anyone you like into your life. Which is part of your problem. Nic apparently has trouble sliding you into her life though. Isn't that a red flag?"

Klara turned back to the mirror, slicked on some lipstick, bit back her anger. She wouldn't lose her temper with Jet. She refused. They were going to have a great night out and Jet would get to know Nic better and she'd see. See that Nic was amazing and wonderful and okay, there were some small issues, but nothing that couldn't be fixed.

"Are you trying to destroy this relationship before it starts?" she said finally.

Jet stood up, came up to her, put a hand on her shoulder. "No, darling. I'm not, I swear."

Klara took her hand and squeezed it. "We need to get out of here or we're going to be late."

THE TAXI smelled of aftershave and cleaning fluid and Klara watched the city fly by the windows. Next to her Jet had been oddly silent. And when she spoke now, her voice was softer than usual.

"I don't want to destroy anything," she said. "I just worry about you. You give your heart away so easily that I'm afraid you're going to get hurt."

"I know. I know you just care."

"I want you to be happy, Klar. I feel... I don't know, I feel kind of responsible for you. It's all that blonde hair and big blue eyes, the whole 'little girl lost in the big city' vibe, I guess."

Klara snorted. "Right, thanks for that."

"You know what I mean."

"I'm glad that you're there for me," Klara said, taking her hand. "And I'm there for you too."

There was a pause as the road crunched under the cab's tires and Klara's heart sped up at the thought of seeing Nic.

"Maybe you're not in love."

"What?"

"I said, maybe you're not in love. Maybe you're just in lust," Jet said.

"And that's supposed to be supportive and to make me feel better?"

"Hear me out. I didn't say you couldn't fall in love with Nic, just maybe that you guys aren't quite there yet. Maybe that's your problem. Maybe you confused lust with love and in truth, you don't really fall in love that easily at all."

"Again, not seeing how that helps."

Jet sighed. "I don't know. It makes me uncomfortable that she doesn't want to talk about a future with you. I get offended on your behalf. Which is weird, I know. But it feels like a red flag. But if you're not actually all the way in love yet, well, then it's okay, I guess. You'll both grow into planning for the future, if you see what I mean."

Klara squeezed her hand again and nodded and went back to looking out of the window.

It was a nice thought. Maybe she wasn't quite in love with Nic yet. Maybe Nic wasn't quite in love with her. Maybe they had something to grow into.

Maybe Nic would one day see that they could be a real part of each others' lives. Maybe Nic would want to move in with her, or want to rent an apartment together, or want to at least invite her to Paris to visit.

It hurt, thinking of Nic so far away. They could do long distance, she guessed. Except, she realized, she wasn't entirely sure if she'd trust Nic so far away from her. She wasn't sure that their connection would survive the distance.

No, this was all ridiculous. She deserved to know where she stood. They both deserved that. And tonight was a great opportunity. They'd have a few drinks, dance, laugh, and at some point, she would get Nic to appreciate that they could have a future together. At some point she'd get Nic to at least acknowledge that this all might work, that they might have something real.

Dare she? If she pushed things then Nic might push back.

On the other hand, if she didn't, then she could be left in this strange limbo forever, not knowing what they were, not knowing how things were going to go.

The cab slowed, steering toward the curb.

Jet let go of her hand.

And maybe they weren't really in love. Could that be?

In the shadows of the pavement she saw movement, and then Nic stepped out, phone to her ear, legs long and slim, hair waving down her back, face animated with conversation. Black jeans encased her legs. A flowing, white shirt shone against the creamy darkness of her skin.

Klara's heart skipped a beat.

No, Jet was wrong. Totally wrong.

There was no way that she wasn't in love with Nic.

And she had to get Nic to admit that she loved her right back. Or it was all for nothing.

Chapter Twenty Seven

The music was pounding and Nic was breathless, sipping at ice cold water and leaning back against the bar. This wasn't her usual scene. In all honesty, she'd have been happier at a smoky rock bar or a salsa club. But Sally excelled at persuading her to do things she normally wouldn't, and she had to admit, the poppy music was kind of catchy.

Sally grinned at her from across the floor and she waved, trying to communicate that she'd dance again later, that right now she needed to hydrate. And rest her aching knees. Danny from the café was around too, jumping and dancing and having a wild time. Jet had come, and was currently ensconced in a booth talking to a man that might or might not be a basketball player, no one had really been able to tell. And then there was Klara.

Klara who had slid onto the dance floor like she belonged there. Klara in her tight jeans and spaghetti strap top and high heels, making Nic's heart pound with lust, making her legs weak and her pulse race. Klara who'd she'd been extra careful with tonight, because she knew if she wasn't she was going to end up bending her over the bar and embarrassing them both.

Klara who was walking toward her.

She drained her glass, turned to the bartender for a refill and Klara eased up beside her, close enough that she could smell the flower and citrus scent of her. Close enough that she groaned with desire under her breath.

"Hey there, bachelorette."

"Hey yourself. Water?"

Klara nodded so she gestured to the bartender. And then she looked over and Klara was looking at the bar and she couldn't help herself, she reached out and put a hand on the small of her back.

"That's the first time you've touched me tonight."

Her mouth dried up. "I thought... I thought we were all clear on that, Klara. It's not you, it's not us, it's just... We have to be careful."

She smiled a small, sad smile. "I thought tonight would be different. It's not like George's family are here or anything."

She was right. It wasn't the thought of someone seeing them that was bothering her. It was the thought of not wanting to stop. And they were in public and... And you never knew who was watching. The heat from Klara's back was burning through to her palm. She took a deep breath, trying to control herself, and then came to a decision.

Grabbing Klara by the hand she pulled her past the bar and around to a shadowy corner and pressed her hard up against a wall. With strong hands she gripped her waist, pulling herself closer and closer until their mouths met and she disappeared into the taste of her. On and on the kiss went, pulsing and pounding and longing, Nic willing herself to meld into Klara's body. Only when she was almost completely out of breath did she pull back, gasping for oxygen.

"Okay..." Klara said slowly.

"Better?" asked Nic, knowing that she was grinning. "I've been wanting to do that all night. And I'm not afraid of people seeing us here. I'm just afraid of starting something that I won't be able to stop. You look... incredible."

Klara lowered her eyes and laughed. "Worried over nothing, huh?"

"Maybe a little," Nic said, knowing she wasn't being completely truthful.

"I'm sorry, it's just..."

"Just what?"

Klara shrugged. "Nothing, it's nothing."

But there was so obviously something that she wanted to say. "Go on, tell me." She reached out and cupped Klara's face. "Tell me."

Klara's eyes were wide and blue and she could swim in them. She was so entranced that she almost didn't hear the words.

"I love you, Nic."

Her brain raced to catch up with her heart, to whisper what had just been said. Then her stomach caught up with the action and flipped over. And her skin prickled into goosebumps. She was... Something. Afraid? Turned on? Flattered? A feeling she didn't recognize, something she couldn't put words to.

"I—" she began.

Then Sally called her name and Danny was coming and she was getting pulled back onto the dancefloor and she watched Klara's pale face as she was sucked back in and honestly, truthfully, really didn't know what she had been going to say in response.

DEEP, CALMING BREATHS. She sipped at a Coke. This wasn't the end of the world. It wasn't Nic's fault. She'd been pulled away from the conversation. She would have said something eventually. But the silence had stretched longer and longer and Klara had had the terrible feeling that she was hanging out on a ledge.

She'd come on too strong.

But it had had to be said.

And now it was out there and...

And nothing.

"Hi, I don't think we've met properly."

She turned and saw a glimpse of blue hair and then a wide smile. Sally. They'd been introduced when she'd arrived, but since then, the woman had been dancing and they hadn't had a chance to talk.

"Sally, right?" she said, putting on her polite face. "You're Nic's best friend."

"One of them. I share that privilege with George," Sally said, pulling a face. "And since you're obviously head over heels for the girl, I'll also tell you that I'm an ex too, just so there's no secrets here."

"Nic's ex?"

"It was a long, long time ago," Sally laughed. "What about another drink?"

Klara nodded and let Sally take her glass. An ex. And a best friend. What better way to find out just what was going on in Nic's head?

"So, um, this whole wedding thing?" she started.

Sally rolled her eyes. "Crazy, isn't it? But that's Nic for you. Mind you, at least there's a fair reason for it, I suppose. Unlike most of Nic's bat-shit crazy plans."

"Bat-shit crazy?"

"Haven't you noticed?" asked Sally. She was already tapping her foot to the music again. "I love Nic to death, don't get me wrong. But she has a serious spontaneity problem. She can't think further ahead than what's for dinner. Like I said though, she is really doing this for George, so I get that there's fair grounds for doing something so insane."

Klara swallowed. "Commitment problems?" she said. "I guess, uh, I guess it must be strange seeing Nic planning a wedding then?"

Sally laughed. "No shit. I don't think Nic will ever settle down. She's a free spirit alright. She—" She stopped for a second, peering at Klara. "Listen, I shouldn't be saying stuff like this if you guys have just started... I mean, you know her, right? It's not like... Uh, are you guys serious?"

If she'd been watching the conversation it might even have been funny. Her drink arrived, she took it. Then she turned back to Sally, not really knowing what to say. Not knowing how to feel. Only knowing that Nic might not be who she thought she was. Knowing that perhaps she was wrong, perhaps there wasn't mutual feeling there, perhaps...

"No," she said, finally. "Not too serious."

SHE PUSHED THROUGH crowds of people, searching over their heads for a hint of pale blonde hair. Sally had told her. Sally had come rushing to find her, said that she might have said something dumb, said that Klara had looked upset, said that she apologized.

And Nic knew she had to find her, but she was damned if she could. She pushed again, against the throng, against the flow of traffic, pushing out onto the street, letting the cool air brush against her skin.

Finally, she saw her. Tall and blonde and alone, waiting at the curb, hand poised to hail a cab.

"Klara!"

When she turned she could see the hurt on her face.

"No," Klara said. "No, please don't. Whatever Sally told you, whatever you think, whatever you want to say, just don't."

"Don't say anything? Don't explain myself? Don't what?"

Klara shook her head. "I know, Nic."

"You know what?" She felt like exploding.

"I'm no idiot. I gave you my heart, but I know you don't want it."

"What are you talking about?"

"You're not ready for me, maybe you never will be. And I can't wait, Nic. I can't hand over my heart and then wait for you to give me yours. I made a mistake. I said I love you and I do. But it was a mistake to tell you, and a mistake to think that you could feel the same way about me as I feel about you."

Her heart thumped. "Klara, you're not giving me a chance here."

"I told you I loved you and you couldn't even respond. I didn't exactly expect you to say it back, but you could have said something.

Could have said that you liked me, or that… Something." Her eyes were filling with tears and she sniffed.

"I want to!"

Klara sighed. "Wanting to isn't enough, Nic. I need more than that. I deserve more than that. And if you're not ready to be in a relationship, if you're not ready to love someone, to plan a future with someone, then this isn't going to work. It's not fair on either of us."

She took a step back now. The F word again. Future. "What are you saying?"

A taxi appeared, orange light glowing. Klara raised her hand and it drifted over to the curb.

"I'm saying goodbye, Nic."

She didn't stop her, didn't say a word. She let Klara climb into the cab, let the door slam, and let the taxi drive away until its lights melted into the rest of the traffic.

Chapter Twenty Eight

The sun rose and she watched the light change across the ceiling of her bedroom. It was barely light when the first message rolled in. She picked up her phone, but it wasn't Nic. Of course it wasn't Nic. It was better that way. Better if they broke all contact. Which didn't make her feel better about it not being Nic.

Klara sighed, rolled over, tried to close her eyes and sleep, but it just wouldn't work. How could doing the right thing hurt so much? How could it feel so wrong to be right? She wasn't even crying, which was a new one on her. Generally, she could be relied upon to have a solidly stereotypical breakup, with crying, ice cream, the works. But this, this was just emptiness, vast and lonely and stretching out forever in front of her.

Another message came in an hour later. And another forty-five minutes after that. Neither from Nic. And eventually she broke down because she had to and texted Jet back. It was a bare ten minutes after that that there was knocking at the front door.

She dragged on some sweatpants and answered.

"You look like hell," Jet said, raising her hands to show that she was carrying coffee.

"And you look like you didn't go home last night," said Klara. Jet was wearing the exact same outfit as she'd worn to the club.

"Eh," was all Jet said as she came inside, handing the coffee over to Klara so that she could unlace her boots.

Klara trailed her to the living room, knowing that a conversation had to happen, knowing that she had to tell Jet everything, but not knowing how to start or even put it into words. So she sipped silently at the coffee and let Jet get comfortable on the couch.

"So, you gonna tell me what happened last night or what?"

"Or what," Klara said, still drinking.

"Fine, I'll guess then. Uh, you got so wasted you forgot to say goodbye to me? No, wait, you got kidnapped and have only just been returned after a mysterious stranger paid your ransom?"

Against her will, Klara smiled a little. "Not exactly."

"Then you should probably tell me." Jet looked over at her. "I was worried, you know. Particularly when no one else knew that you'd left."

"Nic didn't tell you?"

"It was hard to get a word out of Nic, what with all the dancing and drinking she was doing. She wasn't exactly talking sense."

So, Nic had had a good time after all. Despite everything. Well, what had she expected? Nic wasn't invested in a relationship, so of course she wasn't going to let a tiny little break up ruin her evening.

"Well?" Jet prompted.

Klara took a deep breath. Putting it into words was going to make it real. But she needed to make it real. It *was* real.

"We broke up."

There, short, simple, easy.

Jet was already swinging her legs off the couch. "I'll kill her," she said. "I told her I'd stomp her head in if she hurt you, I swear to God, I'll—"

"Jesus, calm down. Where does this obsession with stomping people's heads in come from?"

Jet shrugged, still on the edge of her seat. "Sounds terrifying. I wouldn't actually go through with it. Probably. But that doesn't mean that I won't protect you, Klar. I'll... I don't know. But I won't let her get away with this."

Klara reached out to pat Jet's leg. "Down, boy," she said. "I don't need protecting."

"Of course you do. Little girl lost in the big city and all that, remember?"

Klara did remember. But now the thought irked her. "I'm not a little girl. I'm a woman. An independent woman who can look after herself." It sounded harsh like that. "Mostly," she added.

Jet eyed her for a second before settling back on the couch. "Are you going the round-about way to telling me that you broke up with her? Not the other way around?"

Klara nodded, eyes still dry, hands still steady as she lifted her coffee cup to her lips.

"Why?"

"Because you were right," she said simply.

"As much as I love being right, I might need a little more to go on than that. Right about what exactly?"

"Everything."

Jet lifted an elegant eyebrow and Klara shook herself. She needed to do better here, she needed to put all of this into words.

"I'm naïve," she said. "I give my heart away too easily and all that happens is that I end up getting hurt. I get hurt because I come on too strong, because I become overwhelming, and because I expect other people to feel the exact same way that I do."

Jet frowned at this. "Do you honestly think that?"

"Nic had no plans for me in her future, you were right. I honestly don't think it had even occurred to her to think about it. She refused to discuss anything that would take place after the wedding, like that was a huge defining point in her life, even though it's not real. Her best friend told me that she can't plan further ahead than what's for dinner."

"Okay," Jet said slowly. "So she has commitment problems. They're not insurmountable, you know."

"They are," Klara said. The hurt was burning inside her again now, just as fresh, just as real. "They are insurmountable."

"Why?"

"Because I said it," she burst out. "I told her I love you, I said the words and do you know what she said back?"

She could hear the sound of Jet swallowing as she shook her head.

"Nothing. Not a thing. Not I like you, not I love you, not that's a little too soon, just nothing."

"But Klara—"

"No, there's no buts here. She didn't feel the same way, doesn't feel the same way. I do this every time. I paint a picture of the future that I want with someone that I don't even know. And then when their picture is different from mine, I get hurt. And I'm tired of it. Sick and tired of it."

Jet said nothing. She pulled at Klara's arm, practically dragging her up to the couch, then putting an arm around her. Klara let her head drop down onto Jet's shoulder.

"I have to stop this," she said. "I have to stop falling in love and being naïve. I need to grow up. Maybe you're right, maybe I am a lost little girl in the big city. But it's time I grew up and made some decent decisions. And my first decision is that I'm not falling in love again."

"You sure about that?"

"Yes. I'm tired of being hurt. Let someone else fall in love with me for a change."

Jet snorted. "Not asking for much, are you?"

Klara cuddled in. "I'm asking for what I deserve."

"Took you long enough to realize it." There was a long pause. "Are you sure about Nic? I mean, you fell hard this time. It was one night. Don't you want to give her another chance?"

"Another chance to hurt me? No. I'll be fine. She's in no position to give me what I'm looking for. There's nothing wrong with that, there's nothing wrong with Nic. She's a wonderful person. Just not the kind of person that should be with someone like me, that's all."

"Fair enough." There was another long pause. Jet sounded more cautious when she spoke again. "And the wedding?"

"I should never have gotten involved with it. I'll return the deposit to Mrs. Gainer in the morning."

They sat for a long time on the couch, until Klara's neck started to ache and she had to sit up straighter. She saw then that Jet was watching her.

"I know, I know. All these big girl decisions. I'm more than aware of what losing the Gainer wedding will do to the business."

"Really?"

Klara nodded. It had been a long, sleepless night, she'd had plenty of time to think. "Maybe you're right about that too. Maybe I'm better off out of the love business. Maybe I should start thinking about doing something else."

"Any ideas?"

She pursed her lips in thought. "Well, with the whole not falling in love thing plus the needing a new career thing, the only job I can think of that fulfills my requirements is becoming a nun."

Jet laughed and she was glad. Glad that she wasn't so broken that she couldn't make her best friend laugh. Glad that she wasn't sobbing and sighing all over a box of Kleenex. Okay, it was a different way of handling a break up, but it was working. It would work.

"Why don't you hang on just a little longer before taking your vows," Jet said. "You never know what might happen. You might save the business yet."

Klara doubted it. But then, maybe it was a good thing. Maybe all of this was a good thing. Maybe this was the wake up call that she'd needed.

Of course, it would help if she didn't see Nic's face every time she closed her eyes. She might never sleep again.

Chapter Twenty Nine

The hammering on her bedroom door woke her up. It was loud enough to wake the dead, she couldn't ignore it if she tried.

"What?" she managed to croak.

George stormed in. "I've just had my mother on the phone and..." He slowly tailed off. "You look like shit."

"Thank you so much. You always know just what to say to a girl to make her feel pretty."

He sat down on the edge of her bed. "Seriously, Nic. You look absolutely awful. You can't possibly still be hungover?"

The day before had been a bit of a blur. Everything had hurt, everything had made her throw up, and everything had run together into a haze of water and bathroom and cartoons on the TV. Last night though, last night she'd finally been able to clear her mind, finally been able to think. And it hadn't been particularly pleasant.

"Not hungover," she said. She really didn't want to talk about this. Not even a little bit. It was better to let it brew inside, then let it slowly seep away out of her pores. "A phone call from your mother is never a good thing." Not a great topic of discussion either, but it was the lesser of two evils.

"No," George said. "No, it's not. Especially this one."

"What did she have to say for herself."

His brow furrowed and she suddenly knew without a doubt what was happening here, and knew that George was putting the pieces together too.

"She said that Klara returned the full deposit, that she resigned."

Nic lay back on her pillow. An obvious consequence to breaking up, but not one that she'd actually considered. Fuck.

"And something's happened between you two, hasn't it?" George said. "You and Klara? I should have known it yesterday. Nic, what the hell's been going on?"

"Nothing."

"Hey, this is my wedding too, I think you'd better tell me, don't you?"

"She broke up with me."

There, she'd said it and it was out in the world and real. It didn't make things any better or worse. But now at least George knew. And she'd said it for the first time, so the next time would be easier, and then easier again until before long she'd be able to say it without caring at all.

"Okay," George said. He shifted on the bed.

"It's fine, go ahead, say it. I know you want to say you told me so. Get it out of your system. I deserve it."

He ignored that. "What happened, Nic?"

"We don't need to go into details here."

"I think we do. I think you do. You look like you've had your heart torn out."

"Yeah, right. Not me. That's just not the way I am, okay? Look, I got dumped, it's not pleasant, but it's not the end of the world."

So why did it feel that way? Why did it sting so much? She wasn't ready for a relationship like Klara wanted, she wasn't ready for someone like Klara, she probably never would be. Klara had been completely correct. There was no reason to be so butt-hurt about it.

"How?"

"How what?"

"How did you get dumped?"

She sighed. As much as she loved George, and she did, she'd known that telling him would switch him into full on gossip mode. There was nothing he loved more than a little drama. If she didn't tell him, he'd be like a kid poking an anthill with a stick until she did.

"She told me she loved me. I didn't say anything. Then Sally told her that I never plan ahead, which I'm guessing made Klara freak out about the future, something she's been trying to corner me about for the last few days. Then she walked out of the party. Told me that I wasn't ready for the kind of relationship she wanted. Which is fair enough, I'm not. There. End of story."

George paused for a second. "You said nothing? She told you she loved you and you didn't say anything?"

"Nope."

She'd meant to. In that moment, that horribly scary terrifying moment, when she'd looked into Klara's eyes she'd meant to say something. Okay, maybe not 'I love you.' But she'd been about to admit that her feelings were stronger than she'd suspected. But the words had got stuck and then someone had called for her and the moment had been gone.

"You said nothing," George said again.

"You seem to be a little hung up on that fact," Nic said, shuffling up until she was sitting, back against the wall.

"I just can't imagine..."

And she saw it truly bothered him. "George? Something you want to say?"

He blinked, then looked away. "Last night, Tobias and I, uh, I told Tobias I loved him. He said it back." He looked at her now. "I'm sorry, Nic. Not the greatest of times to tell you, huh?"

She shook her head. "It's fine. Really. That's fantastic. I'm so happy for you, George, really, I am."

She was. It hurt, sure. But that was probably just jealousy, wasn't it?

George sighed. "You know, I hate this. All the lying. It's not me. I mean, it is me. But it shouldn't be. I don't want to do it anymore. Nic, I gotta ask you something."

She forced a laugh. "It can't be a proposal, you've already done that."

His eyes were clear and blue and he looked like a small boy. "I want you to help me come out to my family. Please. I have to do this properly, and I want you to be there. I need you to be there. It seems only right."

She took a deep breath. All this was falling apart. But how could she refuse him? She had to tread carefully now. "I'll help you. Of course I will. After you get your trust fund."

"But—"

"But nothing, George. That money is yours and you know it is. You deserve it and you should have it."

He rolled his eyes. "Seriously, Nic? The wedding is off, you've slept with and been dumped by the wedding planner, I've just declared love to a man for the first time in my life and you still think that we're... That we're what, exactly?"

"I agree that things have kind of... disintegrated. But that doesn't change the reason that I got into this in the first place. Plus, as I'm sure you're dying to point out, I'm kind of the one that ruined everything by hooking up with Klara." Her name tasted funny in her throat.

"But—"

"But nothing. We've been going about this the wrong way. We need to go about this the right way. The *technically* right way."

Everybody else be damned. She wasn't going to let George down, she wasn't going to let him lose out because of her own stupid decisions. She also wasn't going to let him live a lie now that he'd finally had the strength to decide what and who he wanted out of life. And yes, there was still the thought of money in her head, still the thought of Paris, a place to run away to, a place where she could start again. But that was all muddled up in the middle of everything else.

"The technically right way," George echoed.

She took a breath. "Right. We cash out everything we've got and fly to Vegas. Get married, fly back, claim the trust fund because we've fulfilled the conditions attached, and then we get ready for your coming out party. Plus, we might have to start planning another wedding, yours and Tobias's?"

"Nic..."

"Fuck it." She leaned toward him. "We should have done it this way in the first place. Fuck lying to people. This way can work. Who cares if the marriage is a sham? It's not like anyone can stop us doing it. We're adults. Everyone's going to get what they want and we can start divorce proceedings the second you get the cash."

"My mother's going to have a fit."

"Your mother will be so focussed on the fact that you married a Latina that she won't notice."

"Nic.."

She stuck her tongue out at him. "Fine, she'll be so busy wondering how you turned out gay that she won't notice."

"Huh, supportive and helpful as well as devious."

She stuck her tongue out again. He sighed, but she could see that he was bending, flexing, thinking about it. When he finally nodded she felt a weight lift off her shoulders.

"Alright. On one condition."

"Which is?"

"I want to know everything that went down between you and Klara."

She groaned. "I really, really don't want to dissect this, George."

"I know you don't. But it's important. One day you will want a successful relationship, Nic. Realizing how and where you went wrong is key to improving yourself, giving yourself a better shot next time."

She doubted there would be a next time. She'd learned her lesson. One night stands were great, relationships less so. She just wasn't built for them. She didn't trust enough, wasn't open enough, she was too scarred.

"Fine," she said. "But I'm not telling you until we've bought plane tickets. I don't want you leaving me at the altar to run off with your fancy man."

George smiled and his eyes were kind and she knew he wanted the best for her. She just didn't know if she deserved the best.

Chapter Thirty

The bakery was empty and Klara didn't have to wait in line, the first good thing she could remember happening to her for days. She shuffled up to the counter, her regular order on her lips. But before she could speak, the woman behind the counter did.

"A croissant and a latte to go, right?"

Klara frowned, but nodded. "Yes, thanks."

"Not a problem. I'm getting used to the regulars by now."

She turned and put a cup under the spout of the coffee machine. Blue jeans clung to her backside, the strings of her apron emphasizing the curve of her waist. Klara sighed. Emily, that was her name she remembered.

"This place gets so busy I'm surprised you can remember anyone's order," she said, trying to be polite, her hands twitching with the need for caffeine.

Emily turned around. "Oh, I don't remember everyone. But it's tough to forget someone like you."

"I—" She stopped herself, unsure of what to say. The flirtation was so direct it took her aback. Her cheeks flushed. Not out of want, but from a sense of discomfort. She literally didn't know what to do.

"Let me get that croissant for you," Emily said, leaning over and showing a glimpse of cleavage.

She wasn't made of stone. She was heart-broken, sure, but that didn't mean that she didn't have eyes. She glanced down and then looked away. Not appropriate.

"Here we go," said Emily, placing the croissant into a paper bag.

Klara didn't have time to grab it before Emily was pulling out a pen and scrawling something on the brown paper of the bag. Emily turned for the coffee and she pulled the bag toward her.

"What's this?"

"That?" said Emily, turning back with the coffee. She smiled and a dimple danced in her cheek. "That's my phone number. You know, if you felt like calling me. For something. Anything."

Klara's eyebrows shot up in surprise. She felt the familiar beginning of bubbling in her stomach, the first flutterings of something that could be, might be. Then she looked into Emily's eyes and they were blue, not brown like Nic's. She fell back to earth.

"I, uh, I'm very flattered."

"Aha," Emily said. "And very uninterested?"

"It's not that... It's, well, I just, um, I, uh..."

"It's not you, it's me?" offered up Emily with a wry smile. "Or I'm already seeing someone? Or... I'm just getting over someone?"

"That's the one," gulped Klara.

Emily nodded. "My loss then," she said softly. "That'll be nine seventy."

She paid with a ten dollar bill and rushed out of the bakery.

She didn't look back. In fact, she doubted if she'd go in there again. A shame, it was convenient and close to the office. Mind you, she might not have the office for much longer, so maybe it was no bad thing.

It felt like a long time ago when Jet had told her to hold on to her heart. A morning just like this, the first morning she'd seen Emily even, she thought. And Jet had said that she fell in love too easily and that she should try not to, that she should try to keep a hold of her heart for at least a month.

It wasn't that long ago. Weeks, not months. But it had been before all this. Before the wedding, before Nic. The coffee was burning her hand, she hadn't taken the time to put the cup into a cardboard sleeve.

Jet had been right. She usually was. And she was going to do better. She was going to stop being naïve, she was going to grow up, and she sure as hell wasn't handing out her heart on a platter anymore. Screw romance, screw love, screw dating.

She pulled out her keys, unlocking the door to the office and bumping it open with her hip. Wedding dress designs and sample invitations fluttered around her as she closed the door again and thankfully deposited the hot cup onto her desk.

No more love. That was the key.

She used a blush pink napkin to wipe up a drop of coffee that had spilled onto the wooden desk.

IF SHE narrowed her eyes the woman could be Nic. She had long dark hair and flashing dark eyes. The man, on the other hand, looked nothing at all like George. Klara sighed and remembered to smile as the couple pitched in with ideas.

"We were thinking about releasing doves," the man put in.

"Not terribly practical," Klara said, scribbling something down on her pad.

Maybe she should have taken Emily's number. Not to fall in love with, but to try and ease the memory of Nic. Something to try and make her forget the touch of her hand, the softness of her skin. She shivered now at the thought of it.

"And if possible, we'd like sunflowers at the ceremony," the woman in front of her was saying. "That was the first flower that Jack gave to me, so I thought it would be a romantic gesture to feature them in the wedding."

"Out of season," Klara mumbled.

She didn't know if she could be with someone else now. That sounded dramatic, but it was the honest truth. It would feel wrong to kiss someone else, wrong to be in someone else's arms. Like cheating, even though it wasn't and even though she was the one that had ended things. That didn't mean that it didn't hurt.

"We'd prefer shades of pink," the woman said.

Klara lifted an eyebrow. "Really? This season the in thing is white and minimalist, isn't that something that interests you?"

"Not really." The woman pursed her lips and Klara could see little lines around her mouth just like Nic had.

The problem was that even though she'd finished things, even though she knew she'd done the right thing by finishing things, that didn't take away her feelings. She couldn't hate Nic, the woman had done nothing. She couldn't direct her anger anywhere, there was no one really to blame. It was just a relationship that was doomed to failure, one that could never succeed.

She loved Nic, she still did. But even she, the foolish romantic, was smart enough to know that you didn't get involved with someone in the hopes of changing them.

Nic was Nic. She was independent, commitment-phobic, and hated planning for the future. She'd heard that, she'd experienced that, going any further with the relationship would have been madness. How can you change someone who doesn't really want you?

"Well, I think we've heard enough."

The man was standing up. Jack, that was his name. He was wiping his hands on his pants and looking at his fiancée and Klara was looking at the papers in front of her and none of the information was filled out. She shook herself, she really needed to be more with it. Not that she had huge hopes of saving the business, but still.

"We haven't covered catering menus yet," she said.

The couple shared a glance.

"Uh, I don't think that will be necessary," said the man.

"But—"

"No," the woman said, and she was standing now too. "I'm sorry, this just isn't a good fit for us. I don't think this is going to work out."

Klara blinked from one to the other. "If this is about your color scheme," she began.

"No, no it's not," the woman said.

The man sighed and rattled his keys in his hand, obviously ready to get out.

"I'm sorry," said the woman. "It's just... Well, to be honest, it's you."

"Me?"

"You're dismissive of our ideas, you don't seem to share in our happiness. I don't know, maybe you're just not the romantic type," shrugged the woman. "But I really would prefer to work with a planner that was happy to be involved in my wedding. Thank you so much for your time."

Klara didn't have time to say anything. Her mouth was still hanging open as the couple left the office. She sank back into her chair, going over the conversation mentally. Then she groaned.

Jesus. She's been distracted. She could see how she'd given a terrible impression.

She was choosing not to believe in romance anymore. And more to the point, she was infecting others with her negativity. Maybe it was for the best that her business was going down the tubes, she couldn't go on like this.

She picked up her phone, dialing Jet's number, wanting someone to talk to, someone to take the sting out of her day. But the phone just rang and nobody answered.

Great.

Now even Jet didn't want to talk to her.

She put her head in her hands and waited for the tears to come. But they still wouldn't. Her eyes were dry and her stomach was starting to ache and for the first time since she'd moved to the city she really, really wished that she was somewhere else. Anywhere else.

Chapter Thirty One

They suspected nothing until they walked into the living room and saw the figure sitting in the armchair. Nic groaned and dropped her bag of groceries on the coffee table.

"Mom," said George. "What are you doing here?"

"Sit down."

"Is it dad?" George said.

Nic clutched his arm, knowing his propensity to panic. "Sit down," she said, taking the paper grocery bag from him before he dropped it.

"Enough is enough. It's time to stop this little charade. The wedding planner's quit, and I've kept quiet about all of this for as long as I can." The older woman smiled a little bitterly. "Until I finally realized that perhaps you were doing this because of me, not to spite me."

Nic fizzled with anger. "I told you," she hissed to George. "I told you she wouldn't let you marry a Latina, I told you this was going to be a problem."

"That's not the problem," said George's mother. "That's nowhere even close to the problem." She turned her eyes to her son. "George, I love you with all of my heart. You're my son. There is nothing, nothing that you can say to me that will make me love you any less at all. Do you understand that?"

"Sure, mom, of course—"

But Nic nudged him hard with her elbow and he shut up. She was beginning to understand, beginning to think that she might have misjudged Elizabeth Gainer. "Listen to what your mother's saying."

"Take a second just to think about that, George. Please. I will never, ever love you less."

George's face had paled under his tan and he turned to Nic and she could see the indecision on his face and knew that she couldn't do this for him. She nodded, gave him a little smile. "It's time," was all she said.

There was a long silence, long enough that Nic could hear her own heartbeat and really she shouldn't be a part of all of this, yet she was and it was weirdly right that she was here. She could almost hear George summoning up his courage. She took his hand.

"Mom, there's something I need to tell you," he said finally.

His mother leaned forward, smiling, face soft.

"I'm gay."

And now she leaned back and relief flooded her face and Nic thought she saw tears glimmer in her eyes. But she blinked and they were gone.

"You've no idea how long I've waited for you to say that to me," she murmured.

"You knew?" George asked.

His mother smiled. "I've known since you were eight years old. I'm your mother. I've been waiting all these years for you to tell me on your own terms. And then... and then this wedding business started. And still I waited. Until finally it occurred to me that perhaps you were getting married to please me, because you thought that I'd love you less if you were true to yourself, and that just about broke my heart. I couldn't see a way to stop it, not without forcing you to admit something you maybe didn't want to admit."

"And then the wedding stopped itself," Nic said slowly. "Except it didn't."

George's mother turned to her.

"We're going to Vegas. Tomorrow," Nic admitted.

"You see," said George's mother, almost conversationally. "I never had a problem with your ethnicity, Nicolasa. Not in the slightest. What I did have a problem with was you helping my boy play out this charade, you keeping him from being himself."

Anger prickled again. She forced herself to swallow. "You don't understand."

An eyebrow raised. "Then maybe you'd care to explain it to me."

It was George that spoke. "We're getting married so that we can claim grandmother's trust fund," he said, eyes on the ground, looking like a little boy in trouble.

"For the money?" his mother asked. She turned to Nic. "Was this your idea?"

"The money's his," Nic spat.

To her surprise, the woman smiled. "I couldn't agree more," she said. "In fact, if you don't already have tickets to Vegas, I'll be happy to purchase them for you both."

"You would?" George asked, surprise making his voice high.

"The terms of the fund are draconian and out-dated. If all you're doing is getting married on paper to please an old woman, an old woman who, by the way, made my life a misery when I wanted to marry your father, then go right ahead. It's a fine plan. I don't have a problem with that at all. Lying, on the other hand, not being true to yourself, that I can't stand."

"Hold up for a second here," Nic said. "You would have been with us on this plan all along?"

George's mother didn't look at her, she looked at her son. "I want the best for you, that's all I've ever wanted. I want you to fall in love, I want you to love and be loved in return, I want you to be happy. I don't care who that special person is. Are we completely clear?"

George nodded. He was still shaking a little and Nic squeezed his hand.

"And you," George's mother said, turning to her now. She paused. "Maybe you're not quite as bad an influence as I thought you were."

"Uh, thanks?"

"You've still got a chip on your shoulder, don't get me wrong."

Nic frowned at that. For a second she'd almost thought she was being complimented. "Meaning?"

Elizabeth Gainer sighed. "You've had a tough life from all that George has said about you. He mentioned family troubles and I can make my guesses from there. I'm thinking that you're gay too?"

Nic nodded.

"But you're also a grown woman," Elizabeth continued. "And at some point you have to take control of your own life. Stop blaming others for the wrong that was done to you, stop giving others the satisfaction of letting their actions rule you, and start building something of your own. The only person that can decide to make you happy is you. You hear that?"

Nic licked her lips, then nodded. "Loud and clear."

Elizabeth sniffed and stood up. "Fine. I'll leave you to it then. George, use my card to buy the plane tickets if you don't have them already. And call me when you come back. Have a safe trip."

Neither she nor George said a word. Elizabeth reached the door before she turned back.

"Oh, and let me know when you're planning on telling your grandmother. I can't wait to see the look on the old bat's face." She grinned and was gone.

"Jesus Christ," George said as the front door slammed shut.

"Jesus Christ," agreed Nic.

"She knew. She knew this whole damn time and..."

"And you could have told her. Should have told her," Nic said. "And maybe I'm a little bit responsible. I harp on about my own background enough that it's hardly encouraging."

"No," said George. "No, this is all on me. I should have known, I should have had the strength to be truthful, to own who I really am."

"Oh, I don't know about that. It takes time to grow into these things."

"And time to grow out of them," said George, squeezing her hand. "My mother was right. You're thirty-one years old, Nic. This has to stop. The running away, the fear of the future, all you're doing is constantly sabotaging any chance you have of being happy. Even Paris, the only time I've heard you talk about finding a future, that's only about running away again, isn't it?"

"George, I—"

"No, Nic. Take a second, take a look at yourself. You have to want more in life. I know you want more in life. But you're afraid to take it in case it's taken away from you again. But here's the thing, life's a risk. The rewards are great, but you only get them by taking a risk."

"Yeah, but sometimes those risks don't pay off."

She had a shaking, sickening memory. The living room of her parents' house, shutters closed against the bright hot sun, her father's face twisting into disgust, her mother's tears. A memory that she'd shut far away for as long as she could.

"Sometimes they don't," George said. "That's the nature of risk. But sometimes they do. You ever make a dish and it just doesn't turn out right?"

"Sure I do, it happens to every cook."

"Yes, but you don't let that stop you cooking again, do you? That's life. And you know what love is?"

"Enlighten me."

"Love is taking the risk. Knowing that you can be abandoned, that you can lose each other through sickness, life, cheating, circumstances, but taking the damn risk anyway. Because the good parts, the hard parts, they're worth it."

If she closed her eyes she could see Klara's mouth, wide and inviting, lips curling into a smile or trembling into tears or pouting into a kiss.

"Look at you, you declare your love to a man and suddenly you're an expert."

George shook his head and stood up. "You can joke about this all you like, pull out the sarcasm, whatever defensive measures you have. But you know that I'm right, Nic. And I know that Klara wasn't just a one night stand. You wouldn't have risked our friendship, our wedding, our plan for a quick lay. I know you're better than that."

"Klara was—"

"Klara *is* the woman you love. You're the only person that hasn't realized that yet, you know that?"

He didn't wait for an answer. Nic lay her head back against the couch. Her heart beat, her pulse thudded, her brain sparked. The woman she loved. Klara.

The idea was terrifying and very, very exciting.

Chapter Thirty Two

The room was bright and light with large windows overlooking the gardens and fountains below. Nic paced from one side of the suite to the other and back again.

"Jesus, can you sit down already? You're making me seasick." George was lying on a couch, his feet propped up on the arm, flicking through a magazine.

"You're sure they're coming, right?"

"I booked the appointment myself. A bit of a steal for under two hundred bucks, I thought. They'll be here at three. Calm down."

They came to your room. She hadn't known that. She'd envisioned a tacky chapel, complete with an Elvis impersonator, but there were services now that would just come to your room and get the deed done.

Her feet were itching and her mouth was dry. She couldn't shake the feeling that this was all wrong, that she couldn't do this, that there was something off about the whole thing.

"Nic! Sit down!"

She huffed and plonked herself into an armchair.

"Want to tell me what's wrong?" George said, putting his magazine to one side.

"Nothing," she said immediately. Then she said: "Doesn't this seem..." But she didn't finish the sentence.

"Doesn't it seem wrong?" George asked, eyebrow raised. Then he shrugged. "Sure it does."

She closed her eyes. Getting married. It should be a big deal. And truth be told, this was far better than the alternative, which had been a big family wedding and would probably have left her throwing up and making a scene if her present situation was any clue to how she'd handle things.

But when she closed her eyes she saw Klara. Beautiful Klara. Klara in a long white dress, Klara whispering her name, Klara her blonde hair wreathed in flowers. Klara.

In the last twenty four hours she'd come to the realization that she'd screwed up. Screwed up big time. Not because she loved the woman. No, that was the easy part. But because she'd let her walk away.

"It feels wrong because we don't love each other," George said. "Because I love Tobias and you love Klara. That's why it doesn't feel right. A wedding, marriage, it's supposed to be about love."

"Why are you so sure that I love Klara?"

George grinned and swung his legs around so that he was sitting on the couch. "Because you light up when her name is mentioned. Because, other than Sally, I can't remember you spending more than one night with any other woman. But mostly because I can see you now."

She looked down at her battered converse and jeans. "Huh?"

"Not your clothes, idiot. Though on that note I thought you might have chosen something just a little more dressy for your wedding, though those jeans do make your ass look hot."

"They do," she agreed.

"I mean I see you the person. Something's changed in you, Nic. A light's gone out. You're less... I don't know, less energetic maybe. You don't fizz. You're thinking, stuck in your own head, and that's fine, you're working things out, I know that. But I also know that these feelings that you have for Klara are confusing you. Can I ask you something?"

"Sure."

"Have you ever been in love before?"

She shook her head. A week ago, a day ago, she wouldn't have. But now that she'd realized she wondered how she could have been so dumb. But then, this feeling wasn't the gooey, romantic, flowery feeling she'd expected from the movies. It was scary and big and exciting and made her shake inside.

"Why not?"

She looked at him and answered honestly. "I never let myself."

"Hmm, admitting there's a problem is generally the first step to solving the problem," George grinned. "And I think you've just solved your problem as well. You need to let yourself be in love, Nic. You need to give yourself permission."

There was a knock at the door. George got up to answer it and then a man and a woman walked in. One was wearing a suit, the other looked bewildered.

"We're here for the wedding," said the man in the suit. "And this is your witness. Is the living room okay? We can just get ourselves set up, if you'll give me a couple of minutes."

George stood back and let him get on with it and Nic joined him.

"Let myself fall in love?"

"Yep, just jump on into it. Go for it."

She shook her head. "She's never going to come back to me, George. She told me she loved me and I left her hanging. She walked away. She said I wasn't ready for a relationship, I wasn't able to give her what she needed."

The officiant was pulling paperwork out of a briefcase. He beckoned to them.

"If you could just put your full names here," he said.

Nic and George bent to write out their names.

"Then you need to prove yourself to her, don't you?" George said as he wrote. "Show her that you're ready for a relationship. Show her that you can be what she needs."

"Show her that I've changed," Nic said.

"Exactly."

"Uh, excuse me, you're not... you're not discussing forming a new relationship as you're filling out your marriage forms, are you?" The witness was peering at them, brow furrowed.

Nic shared a glance with George and smirked. "Of course not," she said.

"It doesn't matter if you are," the officiant said, all business now. "It's absolutely none of our business."

"So how do I go about doing that?" Nic asked George. "Showing her I've changed, I mean."

"Well, what does she want? Start there," said George.

The officiant cleared his throat. "Perhaps we could begin now."

George looked at Nic. "Last chance to back out."

She grinned at him. "No way, let's do this."

THE FUTURE. The F word. The word that had filled her with dread. That still did a little, if she was being honest.

"How can you be afraid of something that hasn't happened yet?" George asked. His feet were on the coffee table.

"Because."

"Because you're afraid that it won't be what you planned. That it'll be bad," said George. "Which is ridiculous, because statistically there's just as much chance of it being good as bad. And frankly, if you look at someone you love and can't see a future with them, well, you're probably not in the right relationship. Have you tried that? Thinking about you and Klara in the future?"

She sighed and sat on the edge of the couch, closing her eyes. A ridiculous idea. But... But. She could see Klara smiling at someone, could see Klara linking arms with her, she could see the little lines that would radiate from Klara's eyes as she aged, could see the fine blonde hair fading to white, could... She gasped, swallowed, opened her eyes.

"Planning doesn't have to end badly," George said. "And it's about time that you realized that there's more to life than just today. Unless you want Klara for just today, that is?"

She shook her head.

"There you go then. You know that Klara loves romance and you know that she's looking for something real. Show her that you can handle both those things and maybe she'll listen to what you have to say. Maybe you're in with a chance."

So she was supposed to take Klara to Paris now, was she? How would that work? She frowned. No. Paris was running away. If she was going to do this, she had to do it properly.

She didn't need a new start. She needed to build on what she had. She needed to be herself, just... different. She had to stick things out to the bitter end, just for once. And if that meant standing and watching Klara walk away from her again, then so be it. It would tear her heart out, but she was determined that she would finish something for once in her life.

"Can we go to dinner now?" George asked. "I'm starving."

"When do we get the money?"

George raised his eyebrows. "I knew you were a gold-digger, but jeez, that's fast, even for you."

"George, I'm serious. I'm making plans here, and plans need financing. When can we get the money?"

He shrugged. "We can go to the lawyer's office the second we get back, but I've got no idea how long the actual process will take. Not long, I should think. A few days maybe?"

"That's not too bad."

"You'll get your money, Nic, you know you don't have to worry about that."

She eyed him. "I'm not doubting you," she said. "And it's not my money. Not for long, at least."

He stared at her for a second and then shook his head. "I'll let you figure out the details and then you can explain what the hell you're talking about. Now, can we please go and get some food?"

She grinned and let her new husband lead her out of the hotel suite.

Chapter Thirty Three

The first time it happened, she was baffled but flattered. A bunch of white roses, stems long and uncut, presented by a bored looking delivery man who smelled of cheese.

"Who are they from?" she asked.

He shrugged. "Sign here, please."

He handed her a clipboard and she found no further information. And when she put the flowers into a vase she found no card. She put them on the corner of her desk and sat back, looking at them like they might provide some kind of clue.

A grateful client perhaps? It wasn't like she'd had a whole ton of those recently. In fact, she'd turned down the couple of new clients that had come in over the last two weeks. There was no point taking them on. The business was winding down. And she was coming up with a new plan.

No, that wasn't exactly true. She was trying to come up with a new plan. But she was damned if she could think of what she wanted to do, or could do, or was qualified to do.

The bell at the office door rang again and with a sigh she got up to open it. When the door swung back she was faced with a display of wild-flowers so large that she couldn't see the delivery person behind them.

"Just sign here, ma'am," said a disembodied voice, a hand appearing holding a clipboard.

She did as she was told and took the flowers, intrigued now but also a little worried. Who sends two bunches of flowers? Was she dead and no one had told her? Was this some kind of joke? She found another vase and sat the flowers in it, putting it on the windowsill this time.

Did she regret getting involved with Nic?

It was a question that she asked herself a lot. She should. Somehow, the relationship had left her with a failing business and an empty, hollow feeling inside. It had changed her, made her less naïve, less romantic, less everything. Surely a relationship was supposed to make you feel more of a person, not less of one?

But then she couldn't. Because she'd gone in with an open heart and open eyes and, if she was truthful with herself, she would do it all again in a heartbeat. Those few, secret, private meetings had made her feel so complete, so perfect, that she couldn't regret them. She could only regret that she would never have anything like them again.

Perfect, that was part of the problem. She always wanted perfection. Love, as Jet frequently tried to remind her, wasn't about perfection. It was anything but. It was accepting the bad as well as the good, the hair in the shower as well as the Valentine's chocolates.

So no, whatever the consequences, she didn't regret getting involved. She couldn't imagine never having had this experience, like going through life never having taking a breath.

Another knock. With gritted teeth she got up and opened the door and this time there were big, yellow flowers, joyful and open and she signed for them and put them into yet another vase and stood them on the other side of the windowsill and something was going on here. Something weird. Something that wasn't exactly wrong, but that didn't feel right either.

Her office was starting to smell like a nursery.

She jumped as the phone rang.

"At least it's not the damn door," she muttered to herself as she picked up. "Hello?"

"Hi, is that Klara Sorensson? Of Sorensson Wedding Designs?"

"Speaking. How can I help?"

She hoped it wasn't a potential bride, she hated turning them down, hated saying that she wouldn't be able to handle their wedding. Maybe, she thought, as she looked around the office, she could become a florist. Did florists need training? Would she need a degree?

"I was just wondering if I could ask you a few questions, get a few quotes maybe?"

"Uh, what?"

"You know, for the site. Sorry, I should have introduced myself. I'm Sarah White, I'm part of the publicity team with the site and was wondering if I could get a little more info from you. You know, as one of our biggest success stories to date?"

Klara sat down. It was the only thing she could think of to do. She had no idea who this woman was or what she wanted. What the hell kind of success story was she?

"I'm sorry. I think you might have the wrong number." It was a good guess, the only sensible explanation for this.

"I'm sure I don't," the woman said more cautiously. "You're Klara Sorensson."

"Yes."

"Of Sorensson Wedding Designs."

"Yes."

"In which case, if it's not too much trouble, it would be great if you could give me a few quotes. I can send over some questions by email if you prefer. And then I'll just need you to sign a paper giving me permission to use your quotes on the site. It'll be a few minutes of your time, that's all."

Site. She kept saying that word and Klara realized that she had no idea what it really meant, and that it might be key to this entire conversation.

"What site?"

There was a long pause. "LocalVest."

Yet another long pause as Klara took this information in, rolled it around her head and made no sense of it whatsoever.

"Ms. Sorensson, if I may, can I suggest that perhaps you check your LocalVest account? I'll send over an email with those questions and you can decide if you'd like to answer them or not."

"Yes, of course," she said weakly.

Still not a clue what was going on. The woman hung up and the doorbell rang again. Like a zombie, Klara stood up and answered the door. She took the bunch of carnations and signed for them without saying a word. They went on the small coffee table. At least this time they'd come in a vase, she'd have had to put them into a coffee mug otherwise.

The only thing she could do was exactly what the woman had said. So she sat at her desk, logged into her account, and then rubbed her eyes. And rubbed them again.

A five figure balance.

Enough... Enough to get an assistant, enough to push the business to the next level, enough to save the business.

She sat, stomach shaking and breath coming fast for long minutes, just staring at the screen.

She understood now why the woman had called. This was a local investment platform. Investments were pocket change, ten bucks here, five bucks there. This, this was unheard of. And yet here it was. On her screen. Real.

Her first thought was to pick up her mobile and call Jet. But there was no answer. As was often the case these days, Jet was just impossible to get hold of. Scouting other work, finding other wedding planners to keep her from starving and feeling guilty about it, Klara thought. So she put the phone down and started clicking on her screen.

No matter where she clicked though, she didn't find any answers.

The investment was anonymous and had come from one person. That was all she knew.

She was shaking. And she stayed shaking for a solid hour, staring at her computer screen and not understanding how it could be true and getting up to answer the door twice more. Once for red roses, once for a pastel bouquet. Both already in vases, as though whoever was sending them knew that she'd need the containers.

This... this changed everything. Everything.

She was just about getting over the initial shock when there was yet another knock at the door. She gritted her teeth. Looking around her all she could see were flowers. Everywhere. Colors and petals and scents filled the little office. This was getting ridiculous.

But this time there was no floral masterpiece as a greeting.

"I'll need you to sign here, ma'am," said the man, holding out an electronic device. She signed, he grinned and handed her a small box. "Have a nice day now!"

She put the box on the desk. Maybe it was a bomb. She had no idea what had provoked that thought, but the day couldn't get any stranger. She made sure she was sitting down again before she opened it.

Inside were a white envelope and an even smaller box. It was a sign of just how baffled she was that she went for the envelope first. Maybe there was finally some kind of explanation.

Dinner. 7.30 p.m. Tonight.

An address followed.

That was all.

Was this Jet? Was this Jet showing her that romance was still alive, that she shouldn't stop believing? That was the only thing she could think of. Maybe Jet was trying to cheer her up, get her back on track. But Jet didn't have the money for that kind of investment. Unless the investment and the flowers weren't connected at all. Maybe it was just a coincidence that both had happened on the same day.

It had to be Jet. Who else would do this?

Her fingers strayed to the box. She opened it. A sparkle of silver showed from inside. She quickly closed it again. Jewelry. Not Jet then. Or maybe Jet making some kind of pass. She hadn't thought Jet was interested in her, had never had an inkling.

She stared around, her brain fuzzy and confused. There was only one way to find out what all this was. She'd just have to show up for dinner.

Chapter Thirty Four

She did a little spin and George grinned.

"You look fantastic, wife."

Tight black pants, black boots, a white shirt, and the ever-present leather jacket. Dressy enough to pass inspection, she thought, but not too uncomfortable, not too far from who she really was.

"So, you're ready for this?"

"As long as Klara shows up."

There was a shaky feeling whenever she thought about it, whenever she thought that Klara might not, she might have guessed, might want nothing to do with her at all.

"That's all part of the risk, Nic, you know that."

She took a deep breath and nodded. "Thanks."

"You're welcome."

"No, I mean it. Thanks for everything. Thanks for... for always being there. For being patient with me, for helping me realize all this stuff. I don't know where this is going, I don't know what's going to happen, but I do know that you're the best friend anyone could hope for." She smiled and then added: "Husband."

He snorted. "You deserve it, wife. I know that you're afraid. I know that you're terrified. But that's part of life. Yes, people let you down, it happens all the time. But then there are the people that don't let you down. And if you don't give anyone the chance to prove themselves, then you'll never know which is which."

"And I'll die lonely and surrounded by cats that will eat my dead face off," she finished.

"Precisely."

She grinned. "Got it. You're right though, this is terrifying. For the first time I can remember I've actually got a plan. I actually want the future to be here right now, instead of just ignoring it or running away from it."

"Woah there," George said. "Don't waste all those pretty words and thoughts on me. I'm not the one that needs to hear them. Klara is. If she's there. And if she's not there?"

"Then I've learned something valuable and won't forget it," Nic said, even though she wanted to scream at the thought.

"You won't let a failure tonight derail all this progress?"

She shook her head. "No. Promise."

"Hurt we can deal with, pain, heart-break, all of those are the price of admission for riding this ride. You just give me a call if you need me, okay?"

"And you'll come storming over like a knight in shining armor?"

"Um, I'll bring the most expensive liquor I can find at Tobias's and help you drown your sorrows."

"It's a deal." She turned to go, then said: "And bring Tobias. It's about time I met him."

"Agreed. Now get out of here."

THE RESTAURANT was fancy. Not too fancy, but enough that there were fresh flowers on the tables and the silverware was heavy. She just about turned away from the door, not because of her fear of Klara, that she'd already decided to face, had promised herself that she'd do this. But because she wasn't used to being the kind of person that walked into restaurants like this.

The money was theirs, the deal done. She'd done her best with her share and she wasn't exactly rolling in it anymore. But there was enough in her account that she didn't have to worry about the odd nice meal, and definitely didn't need to worry about buying groceries. Enough that she could relax just a tad.

"You have a reservation, ma'am?"

She nodded. "Under Salinas. And a tall, blonde woman should be coming in to meet me, except it's kind of a surprise, so she won't know my name. Do you think you could show her over to my table when she gets here?"

If she gets here, said the voice in her head. Not when. If.

"Of course, ma'am."

"She looks a little like Cate Blanchett. Long bangs, blue eyes, you won't be able to miss her."

The man smiled and his eyes twinkled and already her mouth was watering at the thought of just seeing her again.

She wasn't going to lie. Not to anyone. She didn't know if she loved Klara, no matter what George or anyone else said. But she knew that she wanted to try, she knew that she wanted to go into this with an open heart and honestly, seriously attempt to be the best person she could be. She knew that she wanted to wake up next to Klara, wanted to smell her, wanted to hear her voice when she picked up the phone.

But mostly, right now, she just wanted Klara to walk in through that door.

She checked her phone. Still two minutes to go. She'd been deliberately early, not wanting to miss her, not wanting to wait any longer. She fumbled, putting her phone away in her jacket pocket and then...

"You."

It was only one word. And she knew immediately. She looked up and disappeared into Klara's blue eyes and felt something click into place.

This. Yes. This was right. This was what she needed, what she wanted. She'd never been so sure of anything in her life.

"Me," she said, aware that it was hardly the height of romance.

For a long, long second they stared at each other and Nic knew that everything was going to be okay, that all this was what she was meant for in life.

And then Klara was shaking her head.

"No."

Blood fizzed through her veins. "What do you mean, no?"

"No," said Klara.

Her voice was calm and controlled and she wasn't shouting or emotional or making a scene. Nic looked around the restaurant, wanting to know if anyone else was hearing this, if there was someone else there, if something was happening that she didn't know about. Because this wasn't making sense.

"No?" she echoed, looking back at Klara.

Klara took a breath and blew it out slowly. "No," she said again. "No, Nic. Not this."

"Not what."

She could see Klara swallow, the delicate movement in her neck. "I walked away once, Nic. It was one of the hardest things I've ever done. Because I like you. I love you. I told you I did and that hasn't changed, I don't think it can change."

"Then—"

Klara kept right on talking. "But this, the flowers, the anonymous date, I can't do it, Nic."

"Why not?"

"I don't want your spontaneity. That was never the problem. I don't want the gifts and the flowers and the surprises. I want you. And this all... I don't believe this is you changing, Nic. I don't think this is you thinking about the future. This is you being spontaneous again, and I can't do this again. I can't hurt like this again."

And the words were only just sinking in, but Klara was already walking away, her hips swaying as she threaded through the tables and out of the door and down the street and it was all over.

Nic closed her eyes. This wasn't what was meant to happen. It hadn't been spontaneous at all. She actually had a plan. But Klara had never stopped to listen to it. Klara had thrown love on the table, had smothered her with it and been hurt when she couldn't reciprocate. And now she was trying to reciprocate and she wasn't interested.

Tears were burning in her eyes and the lump in her throat was big enough that she couldn't swallow. She pulled her phone out, intending to call George, knowing that she needed somebody and that she couldn't be alone, not with her heart broken like this.

Then she paused.

What were the consequences here? If she gave up, if she didn't see this thing through then she would likely never see Klara again. Ever.

Or...

Or she could push on, see things through to the end, explain herself. If she could get Klara to listen to her and she still wasn't interested, well, she'd just have to accept that. But it couldn't end like this. Not with Klara not knowing the whole story. That wasn't an end. If she quit now, if she went running back to George, that was giving up, running away.

Klara deserved more than that.

She deserved more than that.

She stood up, practically ran to the door, grabbing her jacket along the way.

"Ma'am, is there a problem?"

The same man was standing at the host desk. She shook her head.

"No, no problem, I just—"

"Is your table not to your satisfaction?"

"It's fine, great," she stared at the door. "I just—"

"Perhaps our menu isn't quite what you were expecting?"

She growled and he took a step back. "No! Everything's fine. I just... I need to find the woman I love, that's all."

And she was running now, pushing out through the door, feet pounding on the street. She needed to make it back to the apartment, needed to pick up the proof that she needed. And then she had to hope to hell that Klara was in her apartment, that she could find her, that she could convince her to talk. Because this had to happen. It had to happen now.

She was going to see this damn relationship through to the bitter end. Whether that end was sixty years from now or an hour. She was not letting this go.

Chapter Thirty Five

It was almost too much to bear. Walking away for the second time, Klara's legs were shaking and it was all she could do to hold onto herself and get out of the restaurant. But she knew she had to go, knew that she couldn't do this.

A year ago, a month ago, the thought of an office full of flowers would have made her heart melt. Just like in the movies. Now though, she could see it for what it was: a gesture that proved nothing other than that Nic had money to throw away. Which she assumed meant that she'd gone through with the wedding.

Well, at least someone had their happy ending.

She wasn't being anti-romantic. She was being realistic. If those flowers had come from someone else, well then, things might be different. But from Nic? As much as she loved the woman, and she truly did, the flowers weren't a sign of anything good.

She made it back to her apartment, which was fortunately flower-free, kicked off her shoes and slumped onto the couch.

Just how was she supposed to do this? How was she supposed to go on every day, knowing that she'd fallen in love, really fallen in love, but that the person she'd fallen for just wasn't the right one?

Maybe she was still looking for that non-existent perfection. Except she could see herself accepting Nic's flaws, she really could. If only there was something more there, something realistic, something that told her Nic was really ready for a relationship. Not a silly romantic gesture, but something real.

Her phone buzzed in her pocket and she picked it up. Spam. Not Nic. Not even Jet, who she'd seen for no more than fifteen minutes in the last two weeks. Jet who she hadn't even told about the investment yet.

She put the phone down again and lay her head back, letting the dark sadness overcome her and finally allowing a tear to escape.

THE PROBLEM with a good cry was that no matter how cathartic it was, the aftermath wasn't exactly pretty. Klara tried not to look at her swollen lips and puffy eyes in the mirror as she splashed cooling water on her face. She took deep breaths, blew her nose, pulled herself together. This was just her life now. She had to accept that. She was going to work, going to build up her business, going to pay back that investment, and she was going to forget all about falling in love with anyone. Ever.

The doorbell rang.

Without thinking, she buzzed whoever it was in.

Maybe she'd get a cat. Or two. Hell, three, who cared now? She could fill the apartment with cats and at least have someone to talk to in the evening.

She was interrupted from her cat dreams by knocking on the door. Crap. Now who could that be? She was in no fit state to be seen. But curiosity got the better of her and she opened up anyway.

"Wait!"

Cracking the door open had been enough to see who it was and she was already beginning to close up again when Nic spoke.

"I need five minutes of your time. After five minutes I will leave immediately if you don't want me to stay."

"Nic, this isn't a great idea."

"Please, just trust me one more time. There's something you need to see."

Cautiously, and much against her better judgment, Klara stepped back. "Five minutes."

"That's all I need," Nic said.

She came inside, sat on the edge of the couch, began rummaging in her bag. And Klara could smell the leather of her jacket, could almost feel the brush of her hair against her cheek. Her legs felt weak and she could almost hate the physical effect that Nic had on her.

"Here." Nic placed an envelope on the table.

"What's this?"

"Open it."

Klara did so. Divorce papers.

"Had them drawn up the week after the wedding, we both did. They're not signed yet, but we're working on it. It shouldn't take much more than a few months for them to go through, the divorce is uncontested."

Klara looked down at the papers in her hands, then back up into deep brown eyes. She swallowed. "That's great, but Nic, I didn't have a problem with you marrying George, not really, I—"

"I'm not finished yet," Nic said, throwing down another envelope.

This time Klara didn't have to open it, she could read the logo at the top corner. "Culinary school?"

"A full acceptance. Right here in the city. I'm staying here and getting my learning done. No need to run away to Paris."

Klara let that sink in, then slowly sat down. Something was beginning to make sense, something was beginning to fit together. A big, anonymous investment, Nic sitting here, Nic getting married and getting money, Nic not going to Paris.

"It was you."

"What was me?" Nic asked.

"The investment. In the business. It was you."

Nic was quiet for a moment, then she nodded.

"I can't pay you back, you know. Not for ages and ages, definitely not for at least a year or so."

"I know," Nic said. "I had an accountant look at things, give me some advice. It's a long term investment, I'm very well aware of that."

"Long term," Klara echoed.

Nic sat back on the couch. "I've been scared," she said. "Scared and hurt and wounded, just like everyone else. But I've been so busy worrying about people walking out on me, that I've never given anyone the chance to stay. I see that now. I see that running away from the future is ridiculous."

"And pretty impossible due to physics and all that," Klara said, feeling lighter by the second.

"Right," grinned Nic. "And running away from the past is just dumb, because it's already happened and it can't un-happen."

"So, barring time travel, here we are in the present," Klara said. She could smell Nic's scent now, could nearly feel her warmth.

"But I can plan for the future. I should plan for the future," Nic said. "Because I want a future. I want to be happy. And mostly I'd like you to be a part of that future. I can't promise that I'm going to be perfect, but I can promise that I'm going to give this my best shot. And I'm still scared and hurt and wounded, but perhaps I can overcome some of those things, because..."

Klara's stomach was doing flips and this was what she'd needed. Nic really was trying, Nic was putting thought into things. Nic had said the word 'future' without pause, without hesitation, without looking like she was going to throw up.

"Because?" she prompted.

And Nic looked at her and their eyes met and very suddenly everything clicked into place. It was like sliding into a warm bed, like fitting in the last puzzle piece, like slipping on a tailor-made jacket.

"Because I think I love you too."

Then Klara was sliding across the couch, was close enough to touch her, but was holding back. Because this wasn't all about Nic. It was about her too.

"I don't expect perfection," she said. "Or I won't. I swear. I know that I have this idea of what love is supposed to look like, and I know that sometimes that's silly. I know that I can be too much, too clingy, too overwhelming. I know that sometimes I need to take a step back from things."

Nic's lips were so close, her skin was so close and Klara could barely speak, could barely form words as her eyes watched those lips move slowly, slowly closer and closer.

"Now is not the time to take a step back," Nic said.

And then those lips were so close she couldn't see them anymore, she could only feel them. She couldn't breathe and it didn't matter, because Nic was in her arms and the pressure of her body was warming her and Klara's insides squirmed with wanting need and then suddenly, it was all gone. Nic was pulling back.

"Sorry, I couldn't help myself. I just had to do that."

"Understandable," Klara managed to mumble.

"So, I've got a proposition."

"You do?" Her voice sounded weak.

"I do. I think that we should be sensible about this, handle this like adults. You have your business to get straight, I have school starting. So I propose that we date one night a week and see where that takes us."

"One night? That's very sensible. Three nights," countered Klara, not doubting at all where this relationship was going now.

"Two," said Nic. "With a review in three months when we can decide whether that's enough or too much."

"Deal."

Nic's hand reached out and cupped her cheek and Klara buried herself in the warmth of it. Was this really real? Could she really believe that Nic was willing to change for her? Or that she was willing to try to change for Nic?

But in the end, did it really matter? What mattered was that they were both willing to work at this. That they both knew that love wasn't easy or romantic or movie-perfect. That it required hard work and they were both going to put in the effort. Wasn't that what all this was about?

Nic's other hand was moving up her thigh. Klara held back a gasp. "And what about after three months?" she asked.

"That's a little far off," Nic said, her eyes on Klara's chest as it heaved up and down. "And I'm a newbie at forward planning. But I'm not saying no to getting married, or moving in together, or getting a dog, or having a kid, or—"

"So you're saying there's potential here?" asked Klara and Nic's hand had reached the waistband of her pants now.

"Oh yes," Nic said, eyes burning with lust. "Definitely potential."

"In that case," said Klara, wriggling now to give Nic better access. "I think we have an agreement."

"That's about the most romantic thing I've ever heard," said Nic as she pushed her hand into the warmth between Klara's legs.

"Oh, haven't you heard?" Klara asked, barely audible now as her breath came faster and faster. "Romance is over-rated. It's forward-planning that really turns me on."

Nic's cheeks were reddening and her eyes were heavy and half-closed. "I think I can work with that," she said.

And then there were no more words. Klara couldn't think straight, let alone talk. Nic pressed against her and the world tilted on its axis and she saw stars exploding and hoped she'd never fall in love with anyone else ever again.

Epilogue

There was a shriek and the sound of hurrying feet and Nic rolled her eyes. Seriously? What now?

"The corsages, where are the corsages?"

"By the door, where they're supposed to be."

"And what about the wine, has it been opened already?"

"Obviously. Would you like some?"

"Right now? Are you serious?" George looked at her like she was some kind of mad-woman. "You want me to stumble down the aisle?"

"You can do cartwheels down the aisle if you want to," she said comfortably. Then she took pity on him. "Have a seat, Georgie. Come on. There's plenty of time. Everything is ready, I promise you."

With a sigh, he collapsed onto a chair. And Nic grinned. She couldn't help but compare this frazzled George to the cool, calm and collected man that had married her in a Vegas hotel room. Apparently, love really did make a difference.

"Take my mind off things," he demanded. "How are things with you and Klara? And where is she?"

"She's coming, she's a guest, not a planner today, remember?"

"And there's you casually avoiding discussing how things are going," said George. "What's the gossip there?"

"Nothing."

"Liar."

Nic sighed. "It's fine. We're fine. It's just... Between work and school we barely see each other."

"And whose fault is that?" George said. "If you'd just bite the bullet and move in together then you'd find those scheduling problems all go away. You'll be sick of the sight of each other within a month."

"Not quite the effect I'm trying to achieve," Nic said dryly.

"You know what I mean."

"Yeah, I know, I know. I just... I don't know if she's into it. I mean, I don't know if she wants to."

George raised an eyebrow. "Are you seriously telling me that little miss 'I can't think further ahead than my next bathroom break' is doubting that little miss 'I fall in love at the literal drop of a hat' wants to move in with her?"

"The irony isn't lost on me." She shrugged, trying not to let how much it bothered her show. "She's busy, I guess. But she never wants to sleep over, she never wants to take off on a Sunday afternoon and go do something. She's fine with scheduled date nights, but getting her at any other time is like getting blood from a stone. I think I might just be a habit at this point."

"Bullshit," George said. "She adores you and you adore her, you've just fallen into a bit of rut is all. You need to work some magic."

"I've got a plan. Kinda."

"Tell me all."

But just at that moment there was a rattling of doors and Klara came in, accompanied by both Jet and Sally. Jet had let her hair grow out and it was now punk length and messy, and she and Sally had matching blue stripes. Their hands were linked and Nic felt a stab of jealousy.

The two had started dating after her bachelorette party, and had kept it secret for so long that Nic wondered if they'd really been together all that time or not. Both had protested that after Klara and Nic's break-up announcing their couple-dom was in bad taste. But Nic thought they just liked the sneaking around.

And then there was Klara. She was laughing at something Sally was saying and her bangs were drifting into her eyes and her generous mouth was half-open and she was draped in a long, pale blue dress that made her eyes sparkle and clung to her body in ways that frankly, should be illegal. And she took Nic's breath away. Just like always.

It terrified her that she might be on the brink of losing this. It kept her up at night to think that Klara was drifting away from her. And when Klara came over to kiss her cheek and press herself against her body it was all she could do to stop herself clasping hold of her and not letting her go.

"SCREW ME IF THEY DON'T make the most damn picture-perfect couple I've ever seen," Jet said. She eyed the mirror, ran a finger below her bottom lip to fix her bright red lipstick.

"You would know," said Klara. "I'm guessing they're just as photogenic as they look?"

"Damn right. I asked Tobias if I could use some of the shots in my portfolio."

Klara pulled a paper towel from the dispenser. "Looks, money, they've got it all. Hardly fair, is it?"

"Psh," said Jet. "I'll take a pizza with Sally in our studio apartment over a five star meal with Tobias in his penthouse any day of the week."

"You know, when I told you to swear off men, I wasn't serious."

Jet grinned in the mirror. "Oh, but I was. Sal's the one for me. I'm absolutely, a hundred percent certain. In the words of a crappy movie that I forget the title of, she completes me."

"You complete me."

"Huh?"

"The quote, it's 'you complete me' not 'she completes me.'"

"Not only are you pedantic, you're also becoming even less romantic with time. How is that possible? I once saw you use an entire box of tissues watching Pretty Woman." Jet turned around. "You and Nic?"

"No!"

"Once more, with feeling. You and Nic?"

"Fine."

"Wanna talk about that?"

Klara sighed. "I'm stuck."

"Gonna need more detail than that, babe."

She had to take a deep breath. "I'm stuck. We're stuck. I love her to death and there's nothing I want more than to spend forever with her but I'm so afraid that she's going to run away that I can't move things forward."

"I thought she was better, I thought she was working on her commitment issues."

"She is. But do I have the right to force commitment onto her? Especially when I know that these things frighten her. I want to ask her to move in or something, but I'm terrified that she'll leave me if I do. So I just settle for what we have already, which is lovely but..."

"But not enough."

"Exactly."

Jet scrunched up her nose. "Sounds like you need to take a chance. Take a risk. I mean, she took one when she chased after you, right? Maybe it's your turn now. You can't live an unhappy life just because you're afraid. Talk to her about it, confront her. I don't see that you have much choice."

"I've been thinking about it," admitted Klara. Though the thought of Nic leaving her made her break out in a cold sweat.

"Then get out of here and do it. There's no time like the present."

"You think?"

"You can think or you can act, one of the two. But you're not going to get any answers until you do something."

Jet strode out of the bathroom and Klara followed her.

The wedding reception was in full swing. Gentle music was playing, guests were laughing, glasses were tinkling against each other. And

Klara's heart was pounding and her palms were sweating and she suddenly just wanted to run away.

Her eyes found Nic at last. Obviously she wasn't in a dress. She was in a black suit, the pants cut tight to show off her slim legs, skimming her ankles, the jacket looser, buttoned with just one fastening, a pale camisole underneath making her look almost naked. Klara felt a pulse between her legs. Nic always had that effect on her. Always.

Her mouth was dry and she was shaking. She turned away. No matter what Jet said, she couldn't do this now. Not yet.

IT WAS COOL AND DARK outside, the breeze played with her hair and the stone of the step was cold under her when she sat. She closed her eyes and treasured the silence for a moment. After the rush of the wedding it was nice to be alone for a second, nice to gather her thoughts.

"Hey."

And it looked like she wasn't the only one with that idea. She smiled and didn't even have to look up to know that it was Klara. She would know that voice anywhere. There was a warmth beside her as Klara sat.

"We need to talk, don't we?" she said, startling herself with her bravery. She hadn't meant to do this now, but suddenly it seemed right.

"We do," Klara said.

Nic swallowed and said quietly: "Are we breaking up?"

The second that followed was just that, a second, maybe less, but it felt like an eternity and Nic's heart stopped beating and the world was worryingly silent.

"No!"

In a rush her breath came back and the world turned again.

"That's good," she said, the words not beginning to cover it. "Because I've got a present for you. I feel like we haven't been spending much time together and I know that you're busy with the business and I'm busy with school, but I also know that we both have a break coming up."

"Uh-oh."

She turned and Klara's face looked very concerned.

"We don't have to do anything," she said quickly. "It was just kind of an idea. I thought maybe it was time that we spent some more time together and that we got away from things and—"

"That's not what I'm worried about," Klara said. She looked down. "I, uh, I thought something similar. I've got you a present too."

Nic frowned. "Um, okay."

Klara bit her lip. "Do you have yours here?"

Nic nodded.

"Me too. Okay, on the count of three, ready? One, two, three."

Nic reached into her inside pocket and pulled out the tickets in one swift movement. In exactly the same amount of time as it took Klara to pull tickets out from her purse. Nic stared down at the two envelopes, side by side. She didn't know what to think.

"Uh, I wanted to be romantic. I thought maybe I hadn't done enough, maybe you were missing all that romance you believe in so much, so I got us a trip to Paris."

Klara snorted and Nic for a moment thought that maybe she was crying, then she looked and saw that she was laughing. Laughing so hard that she nearly was crying. Gently, she prised Klara's tickets from her hand and opened them up. Paris.

And she was laughing too.

"You know," she said, as she wiped her eyes. "We think we're so different, but sometimes I think that's not our problem at all. Sometimes I think we're a lot more similar than we think we are."

"Maybe," said Klara. "And if that's the case then there's something else that maybe you've been thinking about too."

"I have," Nic said cautiously.

"About the future," said Klara.

"About moving in together."

Klara nodded. "I was going to ask you the same thing."

Nic scratched her nose. "Well, it's bad enough that we've got four tickets to Paris. I'm not sure how we're supposed to go about living together in two separate apartments."

"We could toss a coin."

Nic nodded. "Or we could, um, look for a place together. A new place. One just for us. A place we could build a future in. Maybe even think about buying rather than renting."

Klara raised an eyebrow and Nic's stomach lurched because she didn't think she'd ever seen anything sexier in her life. "Now who's being sensible?"

Nic looked down. She couldn't let Klara's lips distract her, not just yet.

"I am. Because I want to be with you, Klara. I love you. I've never wanted to build a future before, and then you came along and now it's the only thing I want. I've been feeling like we've been drifting apart and it's breaking my heart."

There was silence for a second, then Klara spoke. "I know, I felt it too. I think it's because I wanted to ask you to move in, but I was afraid of what you were going to say, afraid that you were going to run away. So I didn't ask and then I started distancing myself because it was hard to be around you and not ask for more, but I'd promised to be less over-whelming, less clingy."

"You don't have to be," Nic said. "Over-whelm me all you want. I want that. I love that. All I want is to be with you. You complete me."

"Exactly!"

"What?"

Klara's eyes were dancing. "Just a conversation I was having with Jet."

Nic rolled her eyes. "Let me guess, about Jerry Maguire?"

"Is that what the movie was called?"

Nic took a breath then shook her head. "Who's derailing the romance now?" she asked. "Stay on topic for a minute, please."

"I thought we were done," protested Klara. "We're all decided. We're going to Paris twice and we're going to buy a fancy new apartment."

"Nobody said anything about fancy," Nic said. "And we're far from done."

She leaned in and brushed her lips against Klara's, feeling Klara's body turn in response, feeling her breath hitch.

"Far from done," murmured Klara.

"Oh, I don't think we're ever going to be done," Nic said.

And she kissed her and the night swirled around them and in her head Nic could see this kiss never ending. Could see them old and grey, could see Klara cradling their child, could see the wedding dresses, could see the house with the picket fence, could see the dog, could see their whole future spinning out in front of her. And it filled her heart.

Don't miss out!

Visit the website below and you can sign up to receive emails whenever Sienna Waters publishes a new book. There's no charge and no obligation.

https://books2read.com/r/B-A-SVLH-VMTLB

BOOKS 2 READ

Connecting independent readers to independent writers.

Also by Sienna Waters

The Opposite of You
A Big Straight Wedding
Love By Numbers
The Life Coach

Watch for more at https://www.siennawaters.com/.

About the Author

I've always loved romance, any kind of romance. But growing up, I could never find the exact kind of romance I wanted, the kind of romance about people like me. So I decided to write it myself. My books are about two people falling in love, just like all romances are. But in my case, those two people just happen to both be women. And all my stories have a happy ending, because I truly believe that there's a happy ending out there waiting for everyone.

When I'm not writing I'm spending far too much time online shopping, trying to persuade my cats to dress up, and trying to persuade my wife that I'm not as crazy as I sometimes appear (she believes this about half the time, the other half of the time she just puts up with me with endless patience).

If you'd like to know more about me, or you'd like to stay up to date with new releases, then subscribe to my newsletter here: http://eepurl.com/dOyZBv

Thank you for reading!

Read more at https://www.siennawaters.com/.